KEYS:
Unlocking the Universe

A short story collection

KEYS: UNLOCKING THE UNIVERSE

Contents

Acknowledgements

Cover by Sheri McMurray

"The Eyes Have It" artwork
By princey

"Gus, Unseen" artwork
By Carolee Eubanks

"Can't Hold a Candle To ... " artwork
By Sally Jean Genter

"Phone Home" artwork
By Christopher J. Valin

"Pretty Was Her Face" artwork
By Eugene Ramos

"The Keys to the Kingdom" artwork
By Susan Eager

"Impossible Summer Snow" artwork
By Sheri McMurray

"Welcome to the Crossroads" artwork
By D.G. McMurry, Jr.

Special thanks to:

Fanlib, for being our meeting place

All of our muses,
whomever and whatever
they may be

Our family and friends,
for their patience, understanding, and
willingness to critique the heck out of us!

Introduction

As I sat quietly in the opium bar a few nights ago, absentmindedly trying to separate my celestial self from my corporeal existence and transcend what is widely accepted as reality through an advanced state of consciousness, I noticed a penny on the floor.

Just an ordinary penny. Nothing special. But staring at it, contemplating it, I was all at once struck with a deep knowing, a total understanding, an epiphany, a revelation ... I saw how this one small coin, this copper circle, embodied the entire experience of creating the very book you're holding in your hands, and by extension, how the book itself and the authors behind it fit into the complex puzzle of humanity, the world at large, and the cosmos. I knew with every ounce of my being that this book, this very book, holds the power to bind the universe together and fill every living being with undying light and happiness.

But I forget how.

Anyway.

There's a term that's very well known in the music industry, but also applies to other facets of creativity, the *sophomore slump*. Also known as the *sophomore jinx*, it refers to an instance in which a second effort fails to live up to the standards of the first effort. This is our second effort. Were we worried about a sophomore slump? Not a chance.

When we first gathered together to write *The Artifact: An Anthology*, we were, in effect, a group of strangers drawn together to see if we could do it. To see if a bunch of authors from across the country, with only e-mail and forums postings to guide them, could pool their talents, add a dash of blood, sweat, and tears, and come out the other side with a book you could hold in your hands.

Reining us in wasn't easy. We each had our own style, our own way of working, our own voice, and our own preferred subject matter. To pull us all in and set us to the task of writing a book where one chapter was dependent on another was a Sisyphean task. But we did it. We did it.

So when it came time to write this book, we were much more than contributing authors. We were friends. Some of us had met in Las Vegas. Some of us started chatting on the phone, and eventually we all did. We became more comfortable with each other, more comfortable with giving and receiving constructive criticism. (With criticism, it's always better to give than receive.) And the end result was, I feel, a stronger, tighter, all-around better book. I believe you'll feel that way too. Sophomore slump? Ha!

On behalf of my dear friends and fellow authors Leila, Chris V., D.G., Carolee, Sheri, Susan, Eugene, Chris W., and Jean, I sincerely hope you enjoy the short stories that follow. The key to enjoying them to the fullest is keying into the theme. I can't explicitly tell you the theme (half the time I can't even find my keys), but it may dawn on you when you least expect it, perhaps while singing in the key of F sharp or vacationing in the Florida Keys. (Can I stop now?)

Keep on reading, and we'll keep on writing.

Now where's that penny?

– Steve Boudreault

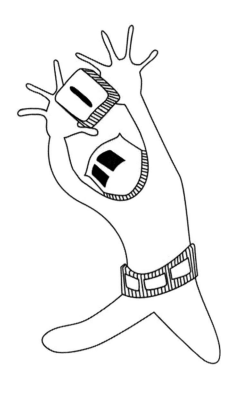

"The Eyes Have It"
By
Steve Boudreault

When we first decided as a group that the common theme of these short stories would be keys, my very first thought was of the keys on a computer keyboard. I suppose that's understandable, when you consider how much of our daily lives are spent typing away. I'm typing right now, matter of fact. See? I just typed that sentence, now I'm typing this one, and another is sure to follow. I'm predicting the future. Freaky.

The plot line of an alien invasion came very naturally, me being a science fiction fan and all, but I decided to deviate from the norm of the human race being enslaved, zombified, vaporized, or eaten, and just have a little fun with it. The first draft was very different from the final, but believe me, the first draft would have been a very, very tough read. Be thankful I left all the letters in.

Extra points to you if you spot the one-line homage to a Broadway show that features a certain mean, green mother from outer space.

Enjoy!

From the online journal of noEYEdea:

It began, as such things often do, on a Wednesday.

I imagine most people remember exactly where they were on that otherwise uneventful morning when they heard that we were officially no longer alone in the universe. I was sitting on my couch, eating cookie dough and watching some daytime television show too embarrassingly awful to identify when the local news anchors cut in, grim-faced and serious, to

3

announce that a ship of heretofore unknown origin and design had landed just outside the Los Angeles Convention Center. Now, when a ship of unknown origin and design lands in the middle of the Nevada desert, covering it up is reasonably simple. But in the heart of L.A.? No weather balloons or swamp gas in this case, folks. This was the real goddamn deal.

The ship was, in fact, from a very far-off world, but of course no one knew that for sure at the time. The circus that built up around it shortly after it crashed rivaled the most lavish super bowl halftime special, with a little Cirqe du Soleil thrown in, multiplied by a factor of ten. You had the people assuming it was a new terrorist weapon and running for their lives. You had the jaded sci-fi types who were convinced it was either part of a movie, or a viral marketing campaign for a movie, and ran home to blog about it and try to find out the deal. And of course, those who believed that Jesus had finally returned in a rocket ship to pass judgment on those who were unworthy to enter the pearly gates. They were my favorite. They made the best signs. One of them had drawn Jesus in a NASA flight suit. Priceless.

What was truly astonishing was the lack of preparedness that became evident in the wake of the landing. Let's face it – every generation since the baby boomers has had some sort of book, movie, or television show to prepare them for what happens when aliens arrive on earth. But there were so many questions that cropped up right away, and no one seemed to have the answers. Should the President go immediately to the landing site in case aliens emerged and wanted to speak to someone in charge? What if there was a danger from the aliens? Should it be the Vice President? An Army general? The Joint Chiefs of Staff? Should the LAPD handle it, or the Marines? Was this considered a national matter or an international one? Should the leaders of all the countries on the planet converge on the ship? What if there were no aliens inside? What then? An endless litany of questions.

The media, of course, immediately set up camp around the ship, and shots of it were all you could see for days on TV, online, in magazines, the newspapers, everywhere. Experts popped up on every kind of program there was, offering up theories and speculation, and reminding everyone over and over that this was the single greatest moment in the history of mankind, irrespective of what was inside that ship.

And that was the most tantalizing part of it all. What was inside that ship? For two days the country – hell the *world* – held its collective breath, waiting for something to happen. That Friday afternoon, something did.

&—┬

The area around the ship had been cordoned off with police barricades, sandbags, and barbed wire. Cops, soldiers, and security personnel kept watch on it around the clock, hitting it with massive spotlights when the sun went down to keep it well in view at all times. Crowds gathered outside the perimeter, at some points ten or twelve people deep, just to get a look at the thing. Scientists set up portable labs and sampled the air and the ground, and swept the area for signs of radiation. Crews in haz-mat suits stood on 24-hour watch.

At 2:34 p.m. that Friday, just before the afternoon commute, the ship gave off a sudden loud whirring noise. Everyone at the scene leapt into action. Guns were drawn, onlookers were pushed back, teams of specialists were moved into position.

The whirring stopped and the area was plunged into an expectant silence.

Then a gasp and a puff of white gas exhaled from the side of the ship, and a hatch swung open. News cameras focused. Cell phones were raised to snap photos. Snipers on surrounding buildings took aim.

From the shadows within the ship, a small figure emerged. It was cute, in its own way – stubby little legs with no apparent feet, shiny alabaster skin, short little arms that ended in round hands with tiny little Tic-Tac fingers, and big, black eyes at the top of its round little face. It waddled out onto the pavement and paused, looking around at the sea of humanity watching it. There was a visible relaxation of everyone with a weapon trained on the little fella. He looked about as dangerous as a teddy bear.

The creature waddled out to a space between the ship and the barricade and continued to scan the crowd. The crowd watched, waited.

Stepping out from a group of Marines in a fortified position, a five-star general named Hadley (whose name would go down in history for what he was about to do) slowly and cautiously lifted a bullhorn to his lips.

"We mean you no harm," he said. The tinny voice echoed in the afternoon stillness. "On behalf of the United States of America, welcome."

The creature looked toward the bullhorn and cocked its head to the side, curious. He waddled a few steps toward the general and his men raised their machine guns.

"At ease, boys, at ease," the general said quietly. The men slowly lowered their weapons.

The creature stopped. General Hadley took a hesitant step forward, right up to an LAPD sawhorse on the perimeter.

"Eye!" the creature suddenly exclaimed in a high, squeaky voice, and more than a few people at the scene jumped in spite of themselves. It had no mouth, but somehow communicated as though it did.

A smile crept across the general's face, and many folks in the crowd smiled as well. The thing everyone feared was turning out to be adorable.

"Eye?" said General Hadley.

The creature suddenly danced from one stubby leg to the other and clapped its hands together like a seal. It seemed delighted.

"Eye!" the creature said again.

The general placed his open palm on his chest. "My name," he said slowly and with great enunciation, "is Hadley." He patted himself. "Hadley."

6

The creature merely stared.

"What can I call you?"

The creature waddled a few steps closer. "Eye!" it squeaked again.

"Is that your name?" asked the general. "Eye?"

Upon hearing it, the creature did its happy dance again. "Eye!"

At that point, even the hardened soldiers and grizzled cops seemed charmed by the small visitor. The people in the crowd craned their necks to see him. Somewhere, a television executive was already drawing up plans for a reality show that featured the alien.

Eye (as we'll call him, for simplicity's sake) waddled in a tight little circle as he scanned the perimeter around him. A few yards away he spotted a woman from one of the science teams typing away on a laptop. He jumped up with what seemed to be joy and waddled quickly over to the spot.

He scuttled under the barrier and headed toward the woman. A few of the soldiers instinctively raised their guns. "Keep those weapons secured!" called General Hadley from the other side of the perimeter. "Do not provoke it!"

The soldiers lowered their arms. Eye ignored all of this and waddled right up to the woman and the laptop.

"Eye!" he squeaked. The woman smiled at him.

"What is it?" she asked.

"Eye!" he squeaked, dancing impatiently on his little legs. "Eye!"

The woman looked at her laptop and then back at Eye. She held it up for him to see. "This?"

This time the alien positively screeched with delight. "Eye!"

The woman laughed, set the laptop on the ground for him, and stepped back. Eye looked over the keyboard and reached toward it with his little arms. It looked as though he meant to type a message of some sort, but instead he began to struggle. With his tiny fingers on the keys, he rocked side to side as he exerted an effort, but to what end no one could tell.

Finally, with a stiff jerk, he pulled a key free from the board, like a dentist extracting a rotten tooth.

He held the key up triumphantly, then spun around and waddled at full speed back toward his ship. "Eye! Eye!" he cried as he moved.

The crowd looked on in confusion. The woman picked up her laptop and looked at the keyboard. The letter "I" was missing.

"I," she whispered.

"Eye!" cried the alien in the distance. He disappeared back into his ship.

The people in the crowd looked from one to another, baffled.

A minute passed, and then the alien reemerged from his ship. But this time, he floated on what looked like a solid, glowing cloud. It appeared much more maneuverable and faster than his legs had been, and he hovered a few feet above the pavement. Behind him, an identical alien floated out on its own glowing cloud. And then another. And another.

The soldiers and police officers brought their weapons up. More aliens poured out of the ship, filling the inside of the perimeter. One after another after another, like some otherworldly clown car.

"Oh dear God in heaven," General Hadley whispered.

The lead alien squeaked "Eye!"

And that's when all hell broke loose.

The aliens flew off in every direction, and the crowd that had gathered broke and ran screaming for cover. More aliens poured out of the ship, dozens, hundreds, a non-stop stream of them. A panicked soldier fired off a shot at an alien that headed straight for him, and suddenly weapons were discharging every which way. Army, Marines, National Guardsmen, police, all firing at the aliens as they flew past and off to who-knew-where.

It was during all of this that they discovered something unique about the aliens' physiology: shooting them didn't have any effect. Their bodies were like jellyfish. The bullets passed right through and the aliens flew off unharmed. And the whole time, more and more aliens flew out from the ship, thousands of them, tens of thousands, all chirping "Eye!" as they flew by.

"Cease fire!" General Hadley cried through his bullhorn, and slowly the gunfire died out. "Eye! Eye! Eye!" cried the aliens as they flew past. Hadley turned to the soldier on his right.

"Major, I want that ship destroyed. We might not be able to shoot them, but we can by-God cut off their source."

"Yes sir!" the major shouted. He grabbed his walkie-talkie. "Unit three, this is base one. We need the tank up here on the double. Over."

"On our way," crackled the response.

A faint rumbling grew louder as a massive tank moved into position at the perimeter. It rolled up as close as it could and turbines inside it whined as the turret swung around.

"Fall back!" the major shouted, and the area cleared. Aliens continued to pour out of the ship, ceaselessly, relentlessly, and the sound of hundreds of them squeaking "Eye!" filled the air.

The major raised his walkie-talkie. "Fire when ready!" he shouted.

A few moments later, smoke shot out from the main gun and a blast of orange fire struck the ship with full concussive force.

Flames licked the ship's hull and black smoke poured from the blast site. It was a few moments until anyone could see what damage had been done, but when the smoke finally cleared, there was no damage to see. The ship was still perfectly intact. And the aliens continued to swarm out the hatch.

General Hadley called the major over. "Can you fire a round into that hatch?"

The major nodded. He clicked his walkie-talkie. "Unit three, hit the hatch. Over."

9

"Will do," came the response, and the tank roared to life again. It rolled to the other side of the ship and the turret swung around and took aim. With a roar, it fired a shell into the ship's hatch, into the heart of the alien swarm. As before, plumes of black smoke obscured the damage.

When it cleared, the ship was still undamaged, but the swarm of aliens had stopped. The silence was shocking after the explosions and the incessant "Eye!" chirping. The last of the aliens flew off down South Figueroa Street.

General Hadley turned to the major. "Major, get me my phone."

The major called over a nearby sergeant. "Whigham! Get the general's phone, on the double! Move it! Move it!"

The sergeant disappeared as Hadley looked slowly around the devastated area. Fire still burned around the ship. Sandbags were torn and poured out. Sawhorses were splintered. Destruction everywhere.

The sergeant returned with Hadley's cell phone. The general dialed quickly.

"This is Hadley," he said. "We have incursions from the crash site. Multiple bogeys with random flight patterns. I want satellite tracking on them, and scramble everything you've got that will fly. We've gotta keep a visual."

He hung up and began to dial another number. As he did, he walked over to one of the science teams gathered around a set of screens with various readouts. "You," he shouted to the team. "Figure out something we can use against them. Acid, napalm, butterfly nets, I don't care. I want a weapon that can stop them."

"We'll get right on it, sir," the lead scientist answered.

The General finished dialing and held the phone to his ear.

"Mr. President, it's Hadley, down at the site." He paused. "We have a situation."

Eric was tired.

It was only three in the afternoon, but he'd been standing at his greeter's station at San Antonio's own CompuTour since they opened, and he was just so tired of saying, "Hi, welcome to CompuTour" to every single person that passed through the doors that he thought he'd soon lose his mind.

As he thumbed through the weekly circular for the thousandth time, he heard the outer doors swoosh open. *Ugh*, he thought. *Just go away.*

He looked up as the inner doors opened and started, "Hi, welcome to … " and stopped dead.

There were half a dozen alien creatures floating just inside the doorway.

" … CompuTour," he finished breathlessly.

The lead creature gazed at Eric with its oversized black eyes. "Eye!" it cried. And with that, the creatures flew in formation down the nearest aisle. Eric followed them at a distance, hypnotized.

Shoppers stepped aside and some cried out as the creatures approached the display of computers on the back wall. The lead alien reached over with its stubby arms and yanked the "I" key from the nearest keyboard.

"Eye!" it cried.

The rest of them zipped around the store in crazy swoops and arcs, forcing people to dive for cover. They yanked out every single "I" key in the store, and then flew right back out, chirping "Eye!" all the way.

Eric spotted his boss crouched on the floor, a look of utter disbelief on his face. "Um … I quit," Eric said.

His boss looked at him. "So do I. C'mon, I'll buy the beers."

On the porch of Zeb's Typewriter Repair Shop ("If You Like Our Work, Hit Return!") in Gallya, Iowa, sat old Zeb, slowly rocking in his splintery rocking chair, muttering softly to himself. Next to him on a small table, an ancient, cracked radio sputtered the news through a tinny speaker.

" … said that while they do not appear to be hostile, citizens should avoid contact at all costs and remain indoors as much as possible. This morning, the Secretary of Defense in a press conference praised the military's response to the quote/unquote invasion, claiming … "

"Heh," muttered Zeb. "Serves 'em right."

Rotterdam Street stretched to the horizon in either direction and passed right in front of Zeb's. It was the main street through town, but today it was ghostly, deserted. A soft breeze sighed through the trees lining the sidewalks, and swayed the storefront signs.

"Serves ya right!" Zeb said louder to no one in particular. "Cain't work yer fancy gadgets now, kin ya?"

Zeb looked up as a solitary cloud passed across the sun.

"Zeb's ole-fashion typewriters alla sudden lookin' better now, ain't they?" he said in his softer voice.

Faintly, from way down on the south end of Rotterdam Street, Zeb heard something.

"Eye," came the sound.

Zeb snapped off the radio and listened more intently.

"Eye!" A little louder now, a little closer.

"Eye?" muttered Zeb. "Eye what?"

Zeb squinted and peered down the street. The swarm of aliens floated along like a high-speed parade, zooming and swooping around trees and lamp posts on their little clouds like tiny stunt pilots.

"Eye! Eye! Eye!" they cried as they bore down on Zeb's shop. Zeb didn't budge. He frowned and squinted his eyes.

"Come on then," he spat. "I ain't afrit o' the likes o' you."

The first wave of aliens zoomed past Zeb's. They flew a few doors down, then, as one, they swung back and hovered in front of the old man and his store.

They stared at Zeb. Zeb stared at them.

"Well?" Zeb said, leaning forward in his rocker.

"Eye!" squeaked the lead alien.

Zeb frowned. "I ain't got any fancy computer machines here!" he cried, shaking his bony fist. "So go on! Git! The lot o' ya!"

The aliens stared blankly.

"Go down the college!" Zeb shouted, pointing toward the north end of Rotterdam. "Them kids all got the machines! Go on! Leave me be!"

The lead alien flew past Zeb and through the front door to the shop.

"Hey!" Zeb exclaimed. "We're closed!"

The alien stayed in the store for a few seconds, then emerged with a rusty old typewriter key. The broken metal stem showed it had been removed with some force.

"Eye!" the alien squeaked with glee.

A dozen more aliens swept past Zeb and into the store.

"I gotta gun!" said Zeb. "An' I'll use it if I hafta!"

The other aliens emerged, each holding a typewriter key. "Eye!" they chirped in unison.

They flew back out to Rotterdam Street to join the rest of the swarm. They headed off down the street, the whole lot of them, and it took almost five minutes for the entire procession to pass by. Their squeaky cries were almost deafening.

After they'd passed, Zeb pushed himself out of his rocker with great strain and great care, and shuffled into the shop. The typewriters on the dusty shelves smiled back at him with gap-toothed grins. Each was missing its "I" key.

"Sumbitch," Zeb muttered.

A woman on the subway in New York City, on her cell phone.

"They're what?" she shouted over the din of the moving cars. "No, I can't – I can't hear you! They're what?"

She listened. "They're stealing what?" A few passengers looked up at her with curiosity, a few with annoyance.

She took the phone from her ear and looked at the display. Lost call. She flipped the phone closed.

A young girl tugged on the woman's jacket. "Was that about the invaders?"

The woman nodded. "A friend of mine in San Diego."

"What did he say?" the young girl asked.

"It was hard to hear him," the woman said, "but it sounded like he said they're stealing things from IKEA."

⊶

On the display board at Denver International Airport:
NOW BOARD NG 5:45 PM FL GHT TO JACKSON, M SS SS PP

⊶

Joel sat on a couch in the Turn Your Head & Coffee shop, completely baked out of his mind. His coffee had been sitting on the table in front of him for nearly an hour, but he either didn't know or didn't care.

Joel's roommate Mary Lou sat across from him, equally baked. She stared at the ceiling with heavy-lidded pink eyes and thought deep, profound thoughts that she knew she'd never be able to express properly. She found that funny. She giggled a little.

Joel leveled his eyes to look at her. "What?"

Mary Lou giggled and shook her head. "Nuh."

Joel shrugged.

14

A few minutes later they heard a commotion from out in the street. There was shouting and a lot of running around, and then the front window of the coffee shop grew dark as the alien swarm flew past.

"There they are," Joel muttered.

"Hm," Mary Lou said.

Joel looked around. "No laptops in here!" he shouted toward the front door. "Move along!" he laughed.

Mary Lou watched the swarm as someone might watch a rain shower on a quiet Sunday afternoon. "I don't want them to take all the I's," she said wistfully.

"Of course not," Joel said. He'd given up watching the aliens and was staring at his sneakers.

Mary Lou became a little more alert. "What do you mean by that?"

Joel sat silent.

Mary Lou sat up. "Hey. I asked you a question. What do you mean by that?"

Joel sighed. "You don't want them to take the I's because you're so self-absorbed," he replied.

The girl's expression darkened.

"What?" she said coldly.

"Self-absorbed," Joel repeated. "Like all your poetry. 'I'm so cold. I'm so alone. Daddy, I know why I don't love you.' Losing the I key for you is nothing short of Armageddon."

Mary Lou looked at him flatly. "For your information, I've won six poetry contests in the last year, I've published my own poetry book, I've been a featured poet in several magazines, and I'm damn proud of it!"

"I, I, I," Joel mocked. He gestured with his head toward the street. "You sound like one of them."

Mary Lou stared at Joel with a rage even the pot couldn't dull. Joel stared defiantly back.

"Maybe you're right," she said finally. "Maybe my poetry should be about something other than myself."

"That would be a start," Joel said.

15

"Okay. How about I write some poems about you?"

Joel snorted. "Go right ahead. Still gonna be tough with no I key."

Mary Lou grinned. "Fortunately enough, there's no I in ass."

⚷

General Hadley stood in the Oval Office, waiting. It had been twenty-four hours since he'd been at the scene, and he knew President Banks would want answers. He just wished he had less absurd ones to give him.

The President strode in with a stream of suited advisors and officials. General Hadley stood at attention and smartly saluted his commander in chief.

"Enough with the formalities, Hadley. I want to know what you know. What are we up against?" the President demanded.

Hadley stood at ease and took a deep breath. "Well, sir … it's an … unusual situation."

"Unusual situation," President Banks mocked. "We have an alien invasion on American soil and you're telling me it's unusual."

"Well, Mister President … I wouldn't classify it as an invasion, exactly."

"Really," said the president. "We're tracking hundreds of thousands of these things all up and down the west coast and moving eastward, and we have no way to stop them. What exactly would you call it?"

"Well, sir, my point is that they haven't actually harmed anyone. In fact, from what we've observed, they appear almost benign."

President Banks stared at him. "Almost?"

The general swallowed so hard he felt his throat click. This was where it started to get silly. "Well, sir, they are causing some property damage. They're ... they appear to be ... "

"Yes?" the president prodded.

" ... stealing the letter 'I' key from every keyboard in the country."

The president leaned back in his chair and digested the information. He seemed to have a hundred questions on his lips, but he asked, simply, "What in the name of God for?"

"We haven't been able to determine that, sir."

"All right, go on. What else have they done?"

"Er ... nothing, sir."

The president's mouth hung open for a moment. "Nothing?"

"No sir. Just stealing the 'I's. Sir."

President Banks leaned forward in his chair and rested his arms on the desk in front of him. He appeared to be considering his words very carefully. "General Hadley," he began, "I have been on this planet for sixty-seven years. I've been a politician for twenty-one years, and President of the United States of America for six years. And that is, without question, the single most ridiculous thing I've ever heard."

The general nodded. "Yes sir."

The president sighed. "General, I need to address the nation a little over an hour from now. Maybe you could give me some idea of what I should tell the American people."

"Sir, with all due respect, you have the finest speechwriters in the country," the general replied. "I'm sure you'll find a way to reassure the country."

An hour later, the president sat behind his desk under bright television lamps and fixed his stare on the camera in front of him. An assistant director to the right of the camera gave a countdown from five, and at zero, the president went live across the country. His teleprompter began to scroll, and the American people watching at home saw a clear look of panic cross President Banks' face. What they did not know was what the president saw scrolling before his eyes:

17

GOOD EVEN NG MY FELLOW AMER CANS …

From the online journal of noEYEdea:

I spoke to a friend of mine in West Chester, Pennsylvania, this morning. He said the I-Guys just swept through and cleaned them out, so their arrival here in Boston is imminent. I want to detail everything I know before they get here.

I saw a report on the news this morning that some of them have started to return to their ship. Evidently the tank blasting the bejeezus out of it did no real damage, and hopefully they're planning to return to wherever they came from and do whatever it is they're going to do with all those "I"s. Good riddance.

No one has any sort of plausible theory about what happened, but there are plenty of implausible ones. My favorite is that we got caught in some sort of intergalactic scavenger hunt. The next planet they visit, they're going to steal all the "J" keys.

Another is that they're really all named "Eye" and each wanted a souvenir of their visit here – like getting a Mickey hat at Disney World with your name embroidered on it.

My theory? They're little pains in the ass who find all of this funny.

I can hear people outside my window. They're pointing up at the sky. And now I hear that annoying, overlapping "Eye!" squeak coming closer.

Well, I'm barricaded in here, so I should have time to finish this before they get to me.

Ah, sh t.

"Gus, Unseen"
By
Carolee Eubanks

The idea for the keys theme came from a game my family played on road trips, when we'd try to take a word and come up with the most convoluted examples of it. We'd also make up bizarre uses for ordinary objects. The idea of doing this as a writing exercise seemed like a fun challenge. Ironically, though, I personally ended up working with a literal, traditional key rather than one that was more outside the box and unusual.

This particular story didn't begin as a collaboration, but it ended as one. Much like Gus in the story, I began the project with the others, human and complete, but began disappearing from the group as the process went on. Gradually I found myself unable to continue, and Steve was kind enough to step in and do a thorough rewrite of the entire second half of the story, breathing new life and meaning into it. He has given it purpose and seamlessly taken these people and situations in a great new direction that feels as though it was there all along, waiting to be revealed. I am in his debt.

⊖—ᴛ

Gus Maddox was invisible. At least, he felt that way sometimes. As he dragged his tattered mop over the hallway floors, just as he'd done for the last twenty years, he realized that the kids thought of him the way they thought of their lockers. A fixture within these walls, non-existent outside them. They grew up, they graduated, and they never looked back … but here he was, still mopping the same floors with the same mop.

It was mostly silent in the school at this time of day. Detention was over and the teachers had gone home, all but a couple of the workaholics who would rather be grading papers at their desks than sitting alone in their empty houses. The team sports practices had just ended, and the remaining sounds that filtered down the hallways were scattered and echoey. Gus made his way along, shuffling with his one thick shoe, one thin shoe, gray oil-stained pants, and shirt a full size too big. Even his clothes made him disappear into the background. The only real indicator of his presence was the keys on his oversized key chain, which rattled as he lumbered painstakingly along.

He always worked on the boys' locker room last. It wasn't the stench of sweaty teenager that made him put off the task, nor the layers of dirt that managed to multiply despite his best efforts. He hated the locker room because it reminded him of who he was, and who he was not. The full-length mirrors along the wall showed him an image he did not want to see, of a graying, fat, aging man who still had not managed to make anything special of his life.

His hair was thinning in addition to turning gray, adding insult to injury. As he glanced up at his reflection, he realized what hair he had left needed to be cut, and could stand to be washed as well. He felt like he looked, the greasy old guy that nobody noticed until there was a spill or a trash can that needed emptying. He ran his hand over the stubble on his cheek and sighed. It wasn't meant to be like this. He'd had more planned than this.

Finishing the locker room without looking up from his work again, he wheeled the mop and bucket into the hall, where he lifted it back onto his cleaning cart. He grabbed the crumpled paper bag off the top shelf of the cart and took a banana out of it. Peeling it open, he stood before the photo wall and looked at the pictures of the school's football teams of years past.

In each one, he could spot the bully. There was always one, on every single team in every single year. One kid who felt it necessary to be cruel to people like him. It had been that way since he was in high school himself, shoved into the lockers he now dusted, by that same one kid, whose face changed on the outside, but whose hate was identical year after year. Was it insecurity that made the bully act this way? Or an overconfidence of some kind? He'd never really understood the motives of the bully, and he wasn't sure he cared to.

Gus stuck the banana peel into the bag and tossed it into the trash can outside the next classroom along the hall. He'd already emptied the trash for the day, and didn't feel like making another trip out to the dumpster. He wheeled the cart toward his maintenance office, really a closet with supplies and a small metal desk that could have come out of World War II government-issue stock. But at least it was his own place to be.

As Gus made his way down the long, dim hallway, he listened to the sounds of his keys jangling, the cart's wheels squeaking, and the faint chirp of his shoes, each making a slightly different sound. Combined, this was the symphony that was the soundtrack to his evenings. He'd never noticed before how comforting the combination was, how soothing the squeaks and jangles and chirps could be. Some might find it scary in the dusk and silence, but he enjoyed the sound.

Just as he had made this realization, he came to his door. Pulling out the enormous key ring, he flipped expertly through, finding the key to his maintenance closet. As he flipped past the others, he paused for a moment at one key. It was an ordinary key, like the others, but slightly smaller. As far as anyone at the school knew, it fit no lock anywhere, but as is human nature, nobody wanted to throw it out in case someone figured out what it unlocked. It had been on the key ring since Gus became a janitor, and since the man before him had first received the ring, or so they said. Nobody was really sure. Forgotten, just like him. Gus shrugged and unlocked the door.

Flipping on the fluorescent light, he wheeled the cart in to its spot in the back of the room. He sighed again, flopped down on the torn-and-taped vinyl-covered chair that was of the same vintage as his desk, and initialed the task chart to indicate that he'd done his job for the day. As if anyone would ever bother to look at it. As if anyone even checked to see whether or not he was in from one day to the next. If he didn't go to the main office to get his paycheck every other Friday, the staff might not even remember he worked there.

Gus grabbed the *TV Guide* from the desk drawer and snapped on the tiny black-and-white television in the corner. He knew he wasn't supposed to have one at work, but nobody had been to his office in so long that he knew he'd never get caught with it.

There was an old episode of the *Twilight Zone* on. He loved watching black-and-white shows on his little TV, because he felt like he wasn't missing out by not having color. Sure, it was a bit grainy and snowy, but the independent channel antenna was only a couple of miles from the school, so as long as he wanted to watch what they were showing, he could watch.

The episode was one he had never seen before, about a mystery in a locked secret compartment hidden behind a shelf in a mansion library. He found the idea mildly amusing. As though there would ever be a hidden compartment just sitting there in a house like that. It was as trite as the old safe-filled-with-valuables-behind-a-painting routine. Bored, he went to change the calendar in the corner over to the new month, realizing as he stood before it that it was now two months behind.

As he pulled the pushpin out of the bulletin board, it fell to the ground and rolled behind a small filing cabinet.

Great, he thought, as he grunted forward to try to reach it. No luck. He set the calendar down and pulled on the cabinet with both hands, jerking it an inch away from the wall. There was the pin. He reached for it, then froze. Next to the pin and the carcasses of what had once been several small bugs and a fly, he saw the dim outline of a door set into the wall, no more than a foot square.

"Oh, come on," he said, looking over his shoulder to see whether someone was there playing an elaborate prank on him. The doorway to the office was empty, as was the room. Only the program continued on in the background, where apparently the police had become involved.

Gus tugged harder on the cabinet, pulling it fully away from the wall. The tile underneath was dull and gray, as though it had not been waxed in decades. He'd never really considered changing the layout of the room, now that he thought about it. There was only one way that all the furniture fit, along with the cart. He realized that it was entirely possible the little door had been there for the whole of his career at the school.

The door had a tiny recessed loop handle. Gus pulled on it, hoping he wouldn't find the corpse of some past enemy of the old janitor's inside, or some old stale contraband of one sort or another. Nothing happened, though. The door didn't give a bit. Then he noticed the keyhole.

Locked, okay, he thought to himself. *Why not?*

He reached for his key ring, planning to see if the school's master key worked in the lock. He stopped before he reached that key, however, when he again came to the mystery key.

Couldn't be, he thought, and angled the key toward the lock anyway.

It fit, and the miniature deadbolt came open with a loud click.

The door still wouldn't come open, at first. He looped his chubby finger around the tiny ring and tugged, hoping he wouldn't pull the mechanism right off the door. Finally, with a squeal, it swung toward him.

The air inside the small boxlike chamber was stale but not unpleasant, like the smell of an antique book. At first glance, Gus thought the cubby might be empty, but then he noticed a brown paper bag shoved into the back, reminding him of the bag that had recently held his banana and now sat in a trash can at the other end of the building.

He reached for the bag and pulled it out into the light. There were no markings on it. He turned it over and over in his hands, then hefted himself up into his chair and set the bag on the desk.

Gus waited a moment to catch his breath from the exertion. He panted a bit and stared at the bag. He noticed now that it was smaller than a full-sized lunch bag, more like a pharmacist's brown bag from decades past. He drew a hand across his forehead to wipe away the perspiration and opened the bag.

Inside, he found a small brown vial, half-filled with liquid, and a note. He gently set the vial next to the bag and opened the note, which was folded once on yellowed paper. The words inside were difficult to read, and appeared to have been written in fountain pen that had long ago faded to nothing. Gus turned on the desk lamp that he almost never used. A burning smell filled the air as the dust on the light bulb cooked away.

Tilting the note this way and that, he squinted and could just make out what it said:

Drink me.

Gus snorted and dropped the note on the desk. "I don't think so." He thought back to the days when this note might have been written, to warnings about brown acid and thalidomide. Whatever nut had put this in the cubby was probably six feet under by now, overdosed no doubt. He sat back and watched the end of his show.

Once Rod Serling had imparted his final words of wisdom, Gus got up slowly and flipped off the television. He'd decided he might as well head home for the night. But instead of leaving, Gus sat back down once more in his chair, regarding the objects on the desk. He picked up the vial and unscrewed the cap, sniffing cautiously at the liquid. It smelled sweet, like sugar-water. Like cotton candy … like a wind-swept pier of carnival childhood. He wanted to taste it. He had to taste it. He absolutely had to taste it right now.

Gus looked down at the stains on his uniform, the dings in the desk, the pathetic existence he called his life. *What do I really have to lose, anyway?* he asked himself, and swigged deeply from the bottle.

The sensation was like nothing he'd ever felt. It was like he was disconnecting from his body, yet he wasn't moving. Like a snake shedding its skin, his self seemed to shift and adjust within him, until the essence that was Gus was like a large, fluffy balloon.

He held up a hand and gazed at it. It still looked the same, slightly age-spotted with dirty fingernails. He stood and reached for the bottle.

And his hand passed right through it.

He tried again. Tried to lift the paper. Tried to turn off his lamp. In each case, his hand went right through the objects, right through the paper, the lamp, the top of his desk like none of it existed. It was as if he wasn't there.

But instead of being panicked or upset, Gus was just … a little bewildered and amused. *Whatever's in that bottle is mighty relaxing,* he thought.

Gus stood up and kicked at the corner of his desk, just to see. His foot went straight through it as well, and there was no sound at all, no sensation of having touched it. A kind of numbness. Gus wondered whether he was dreaming. Or really, really high. Or dead.

Finally, not knowing what else to do, Gus decided to head for home. He walked toward the front door of the school, leaving his door open and his light on. When he reached the door, his hand passed right through the push bar. Gus stared stupidly at the bar, as though it had no right to let his hand go right through it like it did, and he wondered how he was supposed to get out of the building if he couldn't touch anything. Then it dawned on him. He could probably walk right through the door itself.

Gus took a step back and inhaled a deep breath. But as he was about to step forward, a sudden hesitation seized at him, following by paralyzing, irrational fear. What if for some reason he could go out but not come back in? Something in the school had done this to him; if he was going to find answers, he would find them here. He couldn't risk it. He had to stay put.

As he headed back toward his office, he wondered if the liquid in the vial had actually killed him, and being trapped in the school too afraid to leave was his own personal hell. He found the whole thing inappropriately funny, and giggled.

⊷

Gus spent the next few hours wandering the school in utter silence, passing like a ghost through solid objects – desks, doors, lockers, everything – seeking a place to rest. He vaguely missed the squeak of his shoes on the tile.

Rounding a corner, he spotted the teacher's lounge door. Thank goodness – he'd have a couch to lie down on later. But the fridge was a tantalizing handle pull away, and there was no way for him to retrieve the food from it. He found himself glad he'd had the banana earlier. There was no way to know when he'd be able to eat again. Certainly not until morning, at least.

When he made his way into the locker room to look for a stray energy bar, he became suddenly aware of another element to his situation. He didn't notice at first, because he was so accustomed to avoiding the mirror. But there was no escaping it, once he'd seen out of the corner of his eye. He looked, hard, at his reflection. There was nothing there.

"Huh." He smiled a bit to himself. He felt a little relieved, if he was going to be honest about it. Finally, a chance to exist without looking like Old Gus. It was kind of nice.

"Huh," he smiled a bit bigger and headed over to the lounge to get some sleep.

⊷

28

Early the next morning, Gus awoke to voices nearby. He sat up, briefly forgetting where he was. Then he remembered.

"Hey, guys," he said to the two teachers getting coffee. They had their backs to him and were chattering away about something gossip-worthy that had happened. He waited for a lull, then said again: "Hey, guys."

They completely ignored him, which, frankly, was not all that unusual. But Gus wondered whether he was even visible to them, if the mirror had been telling the truth. If it hadn't all just been a weird hallucination brought on by stale drug-water or whatever that had been.

He decided to test it and walked over to them.

"Hey!" he shouted right in the blonde English teacher's ear. She didn't flinch or react at all. He tried to tap the history teacher on the shoulder and his finger went into her body right up to the knuckle. The older lady didn't so much as break her sentence.

This is kind of fun, he thought. *I wonder what they're talking about.* He kicked back on the couch to eavesdrop openly on their gossip.

" … they're cutting jobs again, and who knows who will be next," Mrs. Brown said. "I'm a little worried about the history department."

"Well, I'm sure we'll be fine," Ms. Jorgensen replied. "They can't cut the academic departments any further without hearing from angry parents about it. They'll need to … "

Just then, Dr. Adams from the computer lab came dashing into the room. "Principal Zimmer is on his way in, and he looks furious. Any idea what we did this time?" He looked back and forth between the women in a panic. "I can't lose this job!"

They both shrugged and sat back expectantly to see what would happen next. Gus enjoyed the sensation of sitting in silence among them, their equal.

Principal Zimmer strode into the room, glanced around, and stepped inside. He closed the door behind him.

"We have a situation," he began.

"I really need this job," Dr. Adams pleaded. The look he got from Principal Zimmer silenced him immediately.

"Our situation," he tried again, "is related to our janitor, Mr. Maddox. He did not lock up the school last night, or even close up his office. His light is still on. I've done a quick sweep of the school but can't seem to find him. I'm worried he might be lying ill on a floor somewhere, and I do not want the students to be the ones to come across him. Please fan out and start looking for him immediately, all of you. Notify me the minute you spot him." Principal Zimmer nodded solemnly and strode out of the room.

"Whoa," Dr. Adams said, sinking into a chair. "You think old Maddox finally kicked it? In the line of duty?"

"Get moving, let's find him," Mrs. Brown said firmly, and headed for the door. "I'll check upstairs, Becca, you check the west side, and Adams, try the boys' locker room and restrooms."

They all moved in different directions as Gus Maddox, the person they sought, sat just feet away, watching it all. He laughed to himself a bit. He felt bad that they were going to the trouble, but was surprised and a little touched that they noticed his absence so quickly. He had always figured it'd be weeks before anyone realized he was gone, if he were to be so inclined to leave.

Gus stared absently into space, wondering what was going to happen and how long this condition was going to last. He wondered if he'd be in trouble, lose his job, even, for not locking up. In his own defense, he wasn't physically able to lock up, so ...

His thoughts were interrupted by the door opening again. Principal Zimmer stepped in, quickly, with the vice principal and police officer Michaels, though he was not in uniform. At the moment he just looked like a concerned parent. The three slipped inside and shut the door nervously.

"It's happened again," Principal Zimmer began.

"What? What's happened again?" asked Vice Principal Ruiz.

"The janitor. Vanished. Just like Billy, back, how long has it been now?"

"At least 20 years," answered Ruiz. She and Officer Michaels looked at each other seriously.

"We managed to cover it all up pretty well last time, but how the hell are we supposed to cover up the disappearance of two janitors in the same school?" Zimmer asked, running a hand through his hair. "Look, I grabbed the vial and all the papers from the desk. Looks like he finished his work last night, he initialed the form and all, so this must have happened after."

Gus opened his mouth in astonishment. The reason he'd gotten the job was supposed to be because his predecessor retired, not vanished into thin air! He had no idea there had been any sort of mystery surrounding the last janitor. And the principal knew? And Officer Michaels? And Vice Principal Ruiz, too? Just how big did this cover-up get?

Then Gus closed his mouth again as a new realization came to him. They must never have found the other guy. They'd be acting differently if they had. This condition must never wear off, or if it does, he never came back to tell them, or … Gus' eyes widened as he started to go through all the possibilities in his head. It was overwhelming.

"Let's give it 48 hours or so then call it a missing persons," Officer Michaels began. "We'll do a press conference at his house, post flyers, the usual. And we'll try to find him, but just in case, I suggest you start thinking about how you're going to word the ad for the new janitor," Michaels said grimly.

"Now, you wait just a minute!" Gus stood and shouted angrily. He knew before he did it there would be no reaction from anyone.

8⟍⊤

31

Gus spent the next few days becoming an expert at slipping through all the right solid objects and listening in on all the right conversations. He finally decided that it would be worth the risk to leave the school grounds. The front doors opened and closed constantly throughout the school day, and he figured he'd be able to pass through an open door – hell, he'd done that when he was still solid. He still didn't quite know what he was going to do, but he was able to pass into and out of his house several times. He'd never been so glad to live just a block up the street – he didn't think he'd be able to manage a car door in this state.

So he walked, constantly, from one block to the next, not having any idea what to do with his life, or existence, or whatever it was. It sure felt nice to hear the students and teachers say such kind things about him, though. He learned a lot about what people thought, and was surprised to find that his harshest critic when it came to his appearance had actually been himself. Sure, he didn't like to know that people apparently thought he was a decade or two older than he really was, but they called him old, not ugly. That was pleasant news.

Finally, the afternoon of the press conference arrived. He certainly didn't want to miss it, so he made his way with the rest of the students after school and wandered freely around the neighborhood, waiting for the news teams to gather. A couple of hours later, they did, and he eagerly stood on the sidelines to hear what would be said about him.

"Ladies and gentlemen, I'd like to thank you for coming out here today," began Officer Michaels. Before Gus could hear any more, there was a commotion a short distance away from him, at the very outskirts of the gathered crowd. No one else seemed to be paying attention, but Gus certainly did.

A shy, bespectacled boy of about 14 was cowering by an old maple tree. Standing over him with clenched fists was an older, bigger boy with an expression of distain across his hard features. The bully. Gus moved closer.

"C'mon, you little pissant, fight back," the bully said, slapping the boy hard on the side of the head. The boy's glasses fell to the grass. "C'mon. Little wuss."

The smaller boy fell to his knees and searched around myopically for his spectacles. The bully kicked him hard in the ribs.

Gus felt familiar anger welling up inside him. No one was paying the slightest bit of attention to this punk beating up a poor kid half his size. Forgetting that he was no more solid than smoke, Gus ran over to the bully and reared back his fist. He focused all of his rage and righteous indignation into his punch and swung.

His fist connected with the bully's jaw and shattered it.

The smaller boy found his glasses just in time to see his assailant fall to the ground, knocked out cold. The boy looked around in amazement, and then his face beamed with joy and relief.

But Gus didn't notice. He was in agony.

It was pain like he'd never known in his entire life, and it ripped through him like a lightning bolt. Every atom in his body cried out in anguish as he writhed on the ground and howled like an animal. The pain was everywhere. The pain was everything. He quivered and flailed on the ground just a few yards from the press conference crowd, but no one could see or hear him.

After a few minutes, the pain seemed to abate somewhat. His body still jerked and twitched and tears streamed down his cheeks as he rolled on the grass, seeking a position where he could stand the pain. He breathed as deeply as he could. The pain continued to die down.

Gus rolled on his back and closed his eyes, willing the pain to leave completely, waiting for it to go. After what seemed like an eternity, it did.

Gus opened his eyes and looked up. A man in a dirty tan uniform stood over him, arms folded, watching the press conference. Gus paid him no mind until the man spoke.

"I wouldn't try that again," the man said. He looked down at Gus and offered him a hand. "Pain gets worse every time."

Gus stared at the hand blankly, trying to grasp what was happening. "You can see me?" he asked, finally.

"Yep," the man said, still offering his hand. Gus reluctantly took it and the man pulled him solidly to his feet.

"Who are you?" Gus asked.

The man half smiled, as though he expected Gus to know exactly who he was. "I'm Billy," he said simply.

Gus turned the name over in his head, and then realization struck. "The previous janitor."

"That's me," Billy said.

"You drank that stuff too," Gus said. "The stuff in the vial."

"I had to," Billy said. "Something about it makes you have to. Know what I mean?"

Gus thought back to the moment the scent of the liquid in the vial reached his senses. Yes, he knew exactly what Billy meant.

"Did you put the vial there?" Gus asked. "Was it you?"

Billy laughed softly. "No, not me. That little door has been hiding its secret for a long time. A very long time."

"It has?"

"Well heck, Gus, there hasn't always been a school here, you know," Billy said.

"Oh yeah," Gus said, smiling. "I hadn't thought of that. So … is it just you and me?"

Billy shook his head. "No, not by a long shot. There are many more like us. An entire society."

Gus felt his heart leap. "Where are they?"

"That's … a little complicated," Billy answered. His expression grew serious. "Listen, Gus … there's great work for you if you want it. There's so much more to this than you even realize, than you can even imagine. I can show you."

"Great work … " Gus repeated. He thought about his menial life before everything had happened. A half-existence as a high-school janitor with no family and no friends, with only a black-and-white television to keep him company year in and year out.

"Come with me then?" Billy said, extending his hand.

Gus felt a sudden surge of panic. He didn't know Billy from Adam. Was he just going to run off somewhere with a total stranger? Just because of a promise of great work?

Gus took a step backward. "Hang on, now, hang on … I need … "

" … some time to think it over?" Billy finished, nodding. His expression was one of understanding and a little sympathy. "Okay. Take your time. Call me when you decide. I'll be around."

And with that, Billy floated up from the ground toward the sky. Gus watched, dumbfounded, as Billy continued to float, higher and higher into the heavens, getting smaller and smaller until he was no more than a speck that disappeared into the highest clouds.

The police officers behind Gus continued answering reporter questions, but he hardly noticed. He walked through the crowd and back toward the school in a daze.

⚷

Gus found himself once again in front of the school's photo wall. Kids walked around him, behind him, through him, but he paid no mind. His thoughts were focused on the grainy black-and-white pictures from a bygone era.

He made his way along to the more recent photos, and stopped at one in particular. In it, the football team was lined up in two rows, kneeling and standing, and dead center in the front row knelt Carl Murray, something of a school legend. When he'd been a student, he'd shattered every football record that there was to shatter, and he seemed a cinch to be offered a scholarship and be drafted into the pros. Then, in the first minute of the first game of his senior year, he took a low hit to his knee and tore his ACL. That was it. No more football.

Gus remembered Carl Murray not so much because of his tragic story, but because after he graduated high school, he kept coming back. Every week he would show up on campus to watch the kids practicing football, to talk to all his old teachers, and to gaze longingly at all the trophies he'd won for the school in his time.

Gus realized that he had a lot in common with Carl Murray. After a few years of coming back to the school week after week, Carl reached a point when none of the students knew him anymore. The teachers were still cordial, but some had moved on, and the others were just plain busy. Carl was little more than a ghost, a stranger with a subtle limp wandering the halls, no longer mattering. His time had come and gone, but he hadn't. He was trapped by his own inertia.

If Gus had continued on his path, he would have been little better than Carl Murray. A phantom among the living. A ghost haunting these halls. Gus, unseen by anyone.

But how was his current situation any different? At least before he could get things done, make a difference. Now what good was he? He needed a purpose, a reason for being. He didn't know if Billy's offer was sincere, but it was better than nothing.

Gus headed back outside.

⊖━╾

He found the exact spot where he'd first encountered Billy. There were no crowds now. Gus was all alone, and not quite sure how to proceed.

"Could've just said my name," came Billy's voice from behind, and Gus jumped.

"Scared me," Gus said, embarrassed.

Billy smiled. "So … decided anything?"

36

"I want great work," Gus said simply. "Show me what to do."

Billy extended his hand and Gus took it. All at once Gus was filled with the same lighter-than-air sensation he'd felt when he first drank from the vial. He looked down and saw the ground falling away as he and Billy ascended, higher and higher into the sky. Gus felt a slight tug on his belt as something fell away.

His key ring fell back to earth.

And then he and Billy were gone.

"Light of Dawn"
By
Leila McNamara

The beginning of "Light of Dawn" was a little boy. The main character, Lucien, has been in the back of my mind for nearly a year now, and so I finally made a world to put him in.

What does he do in this world?

Read on ...

＄—┳

A pale, blond boy sat at the dirty window, staring longingly out at the children playing in the street in the early morning light. He had never played a game of *Quitog* before, but he knew all the rules and quirks, because he watched the other children playing it so often. He used to beg to go out and play with them, but he had long given up on that. His parents never let him. They never let him meet the other boys. They never even let him outside.

"Lucien!" Before Lucien had even acknowledged his mother's presence, she had already closed the fading curtains. "You know you aren't allowed to do that!"

Lucien said nothing, staring at the old fabric of the curtains that was now between him and the view of the *Quitog* game. His mother shook her head and walked to the kitchen. Lucien did not open the curtains again, knowing that his mother would likely appear just as he did so and he then would be in worse trouble.

Sighing, Lucien took his fortune stones from his pocket and absentmindedly rolled them around in his hand. His mother had found him with them once before and had hidden them from him, saying that he should not be begging demon spirits to visit him and work their dark magic. Lucien had

39

recovered them quite easily and was unconcerned about what his mother told him. It was just a game, not some demonic ritual, and the only game Lucien had ever played.

He examined his favorite of the stones closely, feeling its smooth shape beneath his fingertips and the slight indentation of black dot on one side of the burgundy rock. This one almost always landed with the dark spot facing the ground, but he hoped that one day his luck would change and it would land face up. It was his lucky charm – it just did not seem to work very well for him.

Lucien did not remember learning this game. He just knew how it worked instinctively. And although it was just a game to him, Lucien knew that the stones did somehow reflect reality – and could possibly affect it.

One of the stones, the dark blue one, once landed with the small line that was carved into it face down. The night that this happened, a great rain had just begun and ended the drought that the kingdom had been suffering for the last season. A few other movements of the stones seemed to reflect what was happening in reality.

He had always doubted that the stones could actually change the future, choosing to believe every little thing that echoed the game to be a coincidence. But the harsh truth was that the stones *did* somehow affect reality. One night a few months before, Lucien's father had gotten drunk and had brutally beaten Lucien, leaving him covered in cuts and bruises and with a broken arm. In the middle of the night, Lucien had thrown the fortune stones across his room while cursing hatefully about his father.

The next morning, Lucien discovered that his father had mysteriously suffocated in his sleep. His mother had screamed so long and loud that a few guards in the city heard and came to their home. Lucien had been locked in his room while they were there, but Lucien had still heard the conversation through the crack under his door.

"You heard and saw nothing?"

"No cuts, no marks … "

Lucien was not allowed to attend the funeral, but he did see his father's body before it was taken from the house. He saw markings on the body's neck – dark red marks that looked like long, lithe fingers – yet no one else could see them.

That had been the only time that the burgundy stone had landed black spot up.

Lucien glanced at the doorway to the kitchen. He wished that his mother would let him go outside and be a normal boy. He had no idea why she did not. It seemed silly. It could not be to protect him – there was nothing to protect him from. Or, at least, nothing that Lucien knew about. But how could he be expected to know anything of the outside world when his only view was through a grimy window?

He wanted to get out there and see the world as it was. He wished to go meet people, learn about the world, and be free from this dull house. Lucien gently shook the stones in his hand. He wanted to have the power to do what he wanted.

Dropping the fortune stones on the dirt floor at his feet, Lucien watched his favorite of the stones curiously as it spun on its side, still moving long after the other stones had stopped. Ignoring how the other stones had landed, Lucien stared at his lucky charm. *I wish I could get out of here.*

A breeze toyed with the locks of blond hair at his neck. Lucien briefly wondered where such a wind could come from inside the closed-up house, but he quickly forgot this thought as the stone stopped spinning, standing up on its side before it suddenly fell down ...

Black dot up.

There was a knock at the door.

Lucien stared at the door intensely. It was rare for them to have visitors. His mother rushed into the room, motioning to Lucien's room. "Go!" Lucien would normally have scrambled to pick up his fortune stones and obediently shut himself away – but this time he simply stared coolly at his mother. "Lucien!" she hissed warningly.

41

Feeling strangely brave, Lucien continued staring defiantly at her. His mother's eyes narrowed and she started toward him, but the door suddenly opened, swinging inward and appearing to have done so without anyone touching it.

Lucien's mother backed fearfully away from the man who entered. He was pale, with a long, dark cloak concealing all of his body except his head, which was shaved smooth. He had a tattoo over one ear of what appeared to be some sort of being made of water.

"Who are you?" Lucien's mother asked, her voice trembling. "Get out of my house!"

"My name is Triton," the man said graciously, despite the manner of the woman before him. He turned to look at Lucien, to whom he nodded politely. Lucien held the man's gaze steadily, finding himself intensely curious about this stranger. He had never met anyone outside of his family before. The man took a step toward him.

"Stay away from him!" Lucien's mother shouted.

"I'm not going to harm him," Triton said gently.

"Get out!"

Triton turned back to her, his bright eyes studying her inquisitively. After a moment, he simply said, "No." And with that he turned around and resumed approaching Lucien.

Lucien's mother shook her head quickly. "Stay away from him! Get out of my house or I'll summon the guards! Leave my son alone!"

Triton knelt before Lucien, ignoring his mother's pleas and warnings. "Do you want me to leave?" Lucien slowly shook his head, seeing no reason to fear this man despite his mother's behavior. "What is your name?" the man asked quietly.

Lucien looked down at his favorite fortune stone and the dot that stared up at him. He slowly raised his eyes to Triton's again.

"Lucien."

"Bringer of light," the man said under his breath, reaching out and touching the side of Lucien's head.

"Don't touch him!" Lucien heard his mother screech. But Lucien did not fear Triton, nor the strange surge of energy that he felt as Triton touched him and muttered something under his breath.

"Yes, it is you."

Lucien wondered what the man was talking about. Triton looked down at the stones and back up to Lucien, his brow furrowed slightly. "*Steen Fortuna*? Who taught you how to use these, Lucien?" Triton picked up Lucien's favorite burgundy stone.

"I did," Lucien answered.

Triton's eyebrow arched in curiosity. "And who gave them to you?"

Lucien shook his head. "I made them."

Triton gazed at him silently for a moment, smiling gently. "Your connection is strong, my lad. It is a great shame we did not find you sooner." Triton turned to glare at Lucien's mother accusatorially as he stood. "Come, Lucien," he said, holding out his hand.

"You're not taking him!"

Lucien reached out and allowed Triton to take his hand. "I am afraid that you have no choice in that matter, madam," said Triton.

"Where are we going?" Lucien asked. Given the expression on his mother's face, he felt he should be afraid of this stranger – but he was not.

Triton smiled down at him. "To the capital of Caym, little one."

"You are *not* taking my son to Orias!" his mother wailed. Triton closed his eyes for a moment before he looked at Lucien's mother again. "That city is full of evil!"

Triton sighed quietly before patiently saying, "Quite the contrary, madam; it is the center of Caym government and society."

"Then the kingdom's government and society are evil," Lucien's mother spat back.

"And that, dear lady, is blasphemy," Triton said warningly. "You already tread on dangerous ground. Keeping the boy hidden all this time? You have been depriving him of his life, his future. You have been keeping him from contributing to our kingdom with his gifts. And he was bound to be discovered. After all, you can suppress the man, but not the Daemon," he said, holding up the fortune stone. "The Daemon *needs* to be found."

"My son is not possessed," Lucien's mother said shakily, her eyes filling with tears.

"Possessed is such a negative term, although essentially correct," Triton admitted. "Come, Lucien. Say goodbye to your mother."

But Lucien simply stared at the woman who had confined him to this dreary life. "I want to go," he said simply. His mother gaped at him in astonishment.

Triton slowly nodded. "Very well."

"You are too obsessed with power, Lucien," Triton scolded. "It is dangerous."

"But I can do more," Lucien insisted. "My Daemon is stronger than you believe."

"You are but an apprentice still. Only a Master Magus can truly know their Daemon. And it matters not how powerful the Daemon is – what matters is how much power they are willing to give to you."

Lucien cursed under his breath, glaring into the orb before him. This was a pointless exercise. Catching glimpses of the future – of one of countless possible futures – was simply not a good way to use his energy and his Daemon's power.

"I know you doubt, young one. You have always doubted."

"Just as you say I cannot yet know my Daemon, you do not yet know me," Lucien replied smoothly. "I do not doubt who I am, nor of who I know I can be. Who I *will* be."

"And who, precisely, will you be?" Triton asked, rubbing his temples as he attempted to keep calm during his apprentice's latest outburst.

"I will be the most powerful of the Magi. I will bring order to the chaos of this universe," he declared, turning his back on Triton. "I will make sure that no one lives as I did," he added quietly.

"You can never have that much power." Triton sighed when Lucien said nothing in response. "You are blessed, Lucien. And I am honored to be your teacher." He put a hand on Lucien's shoulder and turned him around to face him. "Please, Lucien. Trust me."

Lucien dropped his gaze and nodded.

The forests to the north of Caym were treacherous, and many who went in never came out. Rumors of great monsters and powerful necromancers kept most from entering, but it was these rumors that led a cloaked and furtive Lucien to the woods that night. Looking back one last time at Orias, Lucien felt a pang of regret. Triton would be sorely disappointed in him for leaving in the middle of his training. But he had been training for so long, nearly a decade, and he wanted – *needed* – more.

And it was with that thought that he plunged into the darkness beneath the trees.

Lucien cast a perfect spell for light, and he was thus followed by a small, glowing orb that lit up the area around him. He was rather annoyed to find that the trees seemed to have some magic of their own, magic that suppressed some of the orb's light and kept much of the forest from his view.

The sound of the leaves rustling and the branches creaking was unnerving. It sounded as though they were casting their own spells, speaking to each other, perhaps wondering what to do with the unfamiliar being who had dared venture into their realm.

"And you would be right in thinking that."

Lucien whirled around, his eyes attempting to pierce the surrounding darkness and find the one who had apparently read his thoughts. "Who's there?"

"Just one of those you were hoping to meet." Lucien's eyes locked on a pair of glowing red eyes, which appeared to be approaching him. "I am Asmoday."

Lucien forced himself not to shrink back as the speaker came into the light. Lucien had been expecting to meet someone rather like him – a man living with a Daemon. But this was no man, or, at least, not like any man Lucien had ever seen before. Asmoday was at least a head taller than Lucien, and he was adorned with jewelry made of bones, with fangs dangling from his ears and a necklace of assorted smaller bones. His skin was dark and it shimmered oddly, almost as though he was covered in scales.

"Are you afraid?"

"No," Lucien said, managing to keep his voice from shaking.

"Liar." Asmoday took another step forward, his red eyes glinting. "Have you forgotten so soon? I can see into your mind."

Lucien's eyes narrowed dangerously. He was not comfortable with this creature being able to delve into his thoughts.

Asmoday chuckled with amusement. "And now you've shut me out." His face grew serious again. "You came to these forests for training?" Lucien nodded. "From the Necromancers?"

Again, Lucien nodded. "Yes."

"And why shouldn't I just kill you? Why shouldn't I use you as a sacrifice? Or perhaps enslave you in my power?"

"I am a Magus. You cannot enslave me," Lucien said with more confidence than he felt.

The side of Asmoday's mouth pulled into what appeared to be a smirk, although it looked more like a frightening snarl. "You sound very certain of that. But you have no idea what powers I may have."

"I'm not a helpless child," Lucien replied. *Not anymore.*

Asmoday smirked again. "Come." He turned and began walking into the darkness. After a moment's hesitation, Lucien followed, and as they moved deeper into the forest, Lucien noticed the temperature getting increasingly warmer. He wondered if night was already ending, but he saw no sun appearing through the trees above him.

Asmoday waved a clawed hand, and the orb that had been following Lucien vanished, leaving Lucien in complete darkness. He could not even see Asmoday, despite knowing that the creature was merely feet in front of him. "Keep moving, Lucien."

Lucien decided that he hated mind readers – but that he would love to be one.

Asmoday did not kill him. In fact, he took Lucien to his home, which was in the largest tree Lucien had ever seen, and agreed to train him. "You would, of course, be expected to defend us in return, should the need arise," Asmoday said, referring to the cult of Necromancers who studied black magic.

Lucien readily agreed.

Asmoday trained him quickly and brutally. Making an error often resulted in severe injury. Lucien managed to puncture his lung during one trial, but was overjoyed when Asmoday healed him in seconds with little effort. Lucien wondered if Asmoday was even more powerful than he admitted – more specifically, Lucien wondered if Asmoday could bring back the dead.

"Perhaps I can, Lucien. Perhaps, in the future, *you* can."

But responses to Lucien's unspoken questions grew few and far between very quickly as Lucien learned to block all his thoughts from Asmoday's well-trained mind. He was extremely annoyed that he seemed unable to penetrate

47

Asmoday's mind, but his new master did not seem to find this troubling.

"Time, Lucien, time. You can't expect to be all-powerful so quickly."

After a few weeks of training with Asmoday, Lucien finally asked a question that, though it had been on his mind since he met Asmoday, the Necromancer had never answered. "Are you a Magus, Asmoday?"

With his back to Lucien, Asmoday said, "No. A Magus coexists with their Daemon." Asmoday's red eyes gleamed as he turned to look at him. "I control mine."

"That's impossible!" Lucien exclaimed in disbelief. "You can't control a Daemon."

"Yes, that is what you have been taught, isn't it?" Asmoday chuckled darkly. "But controlling another being to *them* … to the Magi … is unthinkable. Not to mention that they believe it is impossible," he continued with a small smile.

"I thought that it was … is it possible?"

Asmoday nodded with a grin.

Lucien moistened his lips. "And … can you teach me?" Again, Asmoday nodded his head, and Lucien smiled. "Now?"

Asmoday motioned to the tree. "Inside."

Lucien bit back a groan when Asmoday revealed that he owned an orb like the one Triton had forced Lucien to stare at for many long hours. "Have you used one of these before?" Asmoday asked, motioning for Lucien to sit in front of it.

"Yes."

"To see into the future? I believe that is what the Magi are taught."

"Yes."

Asmoday shook his head and clicked his tongue. "I never did quite understand that. No Magus I know of is strong enough to discover anything of real value using these in such a way."

Lucien's eyes brightened and he suddenly became hopeful. "There's more than one way?"

48

"Of course."

Lucien smiled, very glad that he would not be repeating the same pointless exercise that Triton had constantly required of him.

"Now, focus."

Lucien was not exactly happy with staring at the orb and wondering what he was supposed to see. "Do I have to open my mind?"

"No!" Asmoday said sharply. "That is the practice of foreseeing that which may be. This is seeing what *is*." Lucien tried to focus on the orb, wondering what he was going to experience. "Search inside yourself, Lucien. Find the other part of you – the Daemon."

Lucien was, for the first time, questioning his new master. However, he attempted to do as Asmoday said. "I can't find it."

"Not it. Him or her."

Lucien glanced up at Asmoday, who arched an eyebrow and nodded toward the orb to indicate that he should still be concentrating on it. "Him *or* her? You don't know?"

"Search for that part of you. You are not Lucien. You are a combination of Lucien and the Daemon who lives in the same body and mind."

Lucien's mouth opened slightly when he realized that he was watching himself going through the dark forests, the orb of light following him. "I see … me. In the forest, before you found me. Why am I seeing the past?"

"You may not be. What you are searching for can appear in many different forms. No two are alike." For a while, Asmoday fell silent. Then he asked, "Have you found them?"

"No," said Lucien. "Wait … " The orb that was following him was taking on a different shape. The light darkened to burgundy, but the figure it had become, now almost humanlike, still glowed.

"What do you see?"

Lucien, the one he was somehow watching, turned to face the form behind him. "Light … dark light."

49

"Dark light … " Asmoday repeated quietly.

"A form. Almost like a man, but … not."

"Is it a he?"

The form suddenly glowed brighter, and Lucien wondered if it was an affirmative. "I … I believe so."

"Talk to him. Ask who he is," Asmoday said, his voice sounding far away.

Lucien did as his master asked, but the form was silent. "He isn't answering," Lucien said after a few moments.

"Can you touch him?"

"He's light," Lucien stated, assuming that fact meant that he could not touch the form.

"I know. But reach out – can you feel anything?"

Lucien reached out and shuddered as he felt a sudden flow of heat spread through his body. "It's hot, it's … " He took a deep breath. "It … it knows my name … "

"He knows you. It's only fair for you to know him."

"He's … he's hiding it," Lucien said as he felt more about the form.

"What can you feel?"

"He's my Daemon." Lucien smiled slightly. "I never thought I would actually … he's old. Very old."

"Go on," Asmoday prompted quietly when Lucien fell silent.

"He's … he's lived with a king. Three centuries ago," he said in amazement.

"Nice … " Asmoday hissed.

"He's been protecting me," Lucien said, smiling. "Ever since I was a young boy." Lucien's mouth dropped open. "He killed my father."

"Was your father dangerous?"

"He beat me," Lucien replied quietly. "The Daemon got rid of that danger … "

"What is he called?" Asmoday asked. "His name?"

Lucien cried out in pain, pulling his hand away from the sudden agony. "When I tried to learn his name, he hurt me!"

"Try again," Asmoday responded. "Trust me. I know it might hurt – it will hurt, much more. But you must learn his name if you wish for true power." Lucien winced as he again reached out to the Daemon. The Daemon appeared to be distrustful of his intentions now, and the contact was uncomfortable. "Learning his name is imperative," Asmoday said in his ear.

The harder Lucien tried to learn the Daemon's name, the more the Daemon fought back and the greater the pain. Knowing that this was needed to gain power, Lucien endured the increasing agony and continued searching for the name. But Lucien was convinced that the pain was only in his mind. He was so close to obtaining the name …

"The name is the key," Asmoday breathed. "Find it."

Flashes of memories that were not his began racing through Lucien's mind. Some of the images were of random people and places, while most were completely foreign to Lucien. Some of the things he saw physically pained him to attempt to understand.

Light … light of dawn …

Lucien cried out in pain as he felt fire flowing through his veins. The pain was nearly unbearable and he began to realize that it was not merely in mind. The Daemon was nearly controlling him, keeping him from the key information Lucien desired.

Bringer of light …

Lucien was certain that he would die from the anguish, but he had to keep trying. The Daemon's response to his attempt at gaining the information confirmed to Lucien that he was close to gaining complete control over …

Zoran.

Lucien felt the fire in his veins replaced by intense power as he thought of his Daemon's name – of Zoran. With his name he could control it, control *everything*. He suddenly knew so much more than he had before. He knew history that he had never before heard of, all the people whom Zoran had ever known, and more than that … he knew how to control more power, and he knew that power was his. He was powerful.

Lucien grinned wickedly.

"'You are too obsessed with power, Lucien.' That is what you used to claim."

Triton turned around in surprise when he heard the voice. "Lucien? My boy, where have you been?" he asked with a smile, his eyes searching for his apprentice, who had gone missing and had been presumed dead.

"I'm right here, Triton. And if you had any true power, you would be able to see me."

Triton saw a shadow move out of the corner of his eye, but when he moved to look in that direction, he saw no one. "Lucien? Enough of these games. Tell me where you have been, and then we must continue your training."

"Training?" Lucien sounded almost amused. "Yes, let us continue with training … "

Triton was unable to keep himself from leaping back in surprise as Lucien seemed to appear from nowhere merely inches from his face. Chuckling quietly, Triton said, "Learned a new trick, have you? Just where have you been?" Lucien's smile was not one that Triton recognized. It was far more arrogant and disconcerting then any smile he had seen on his apprentice's handsome face before. "What happened to you?"

"I've been training."

Triton had no time to react when he was suddenly forced back by an unseen force, his body moving until it impacted the wall behind him in the courtyard. He got to his feet quickly, his eyes narrowing suspiciously as he studied his student. "What is the meaning of this, Lucien?" he asked as he straightened out his cloak.

Lucien was still smiling deviously. "Is there not always a time when the student surpasses the teacher?"

And then Lucien was gone again. Triton's eyes flashed as they searched his surroundings, occasionally catching a brief glance of a shadow or of a shimmer in the air. "And from whom did you receive this training?" he asked, growing apprehensive of Lucien's intentions.

"The Magi have begun to destroy the Northern Forests of late, have they not?"

Confused by the sudden change of subject, Triton slowly nodded. "Yes … the Necromancers were becoming too dangerous. We need to get them out of Caym."

"They are not in Caym. Those forests are their own. The Magi's claim on that land is not valid."

Triton's brow furrowed with suspicion. "Why are you suddenly so concerned with those beings? They are dangerous and evil."

"No!" Lucien said sharply. "You are merely afraid of them because you know that they have more power than you."

Triton's eyes narrowed slightly. "What happened while you were away, Lucien? Where were you?"

"Pull out your armies from the Forests."

Triton's mouth fell open, shocked by the demand. "Lucien, the Necromancers are evil – "

"No, they are not. Order everyone to retreat from the Forests," Lucien again demanded.

"I do not have that much power," Triton said slowly.

"You are one of five in control of Caym – I'm sure that you can sway the others to your point of view."

The air around Triton felt strangely cold. He began to prepare to use some of his Daemon's power, growing very anxious. Lucien was not behaving like himself, and defending the Necromancers was so out of character for any Magus. "No. I will not."

During the silence that followed, Triton wondered if Lucien had left without his knowledge. But then he felt something sharp against his throat. "Then it is time for new leadership in this land."

Lucien looked from the bloodied stone knife in his hands and then into the lifeless eyes of his former master. Triton had been a good teacher, but he was limited, trapped in old ways of thinking. That was why Lucien had sought out Asmoday, and the Necromancer had helped him obtain more power than he had ever imagined being able to control.

The Magi had decided to force the Necromancers from their land, claiming them to be treacherous and evil, which was a complete lie. And Lucien now fought for them, defended them, and was now earning them control over the lands that the Magi had long ruled over.

"You did this," Lucien said to the limp body in his arms. "You made this happen. You allowed yourself to bow to your Daemon." Lucien watched with fascination as the tattoo on Triton's head began to move. "To you, *Vepar*," Lucien hissed, the name rolling off his tongue as though he had known it all his life.

Although all breath had left Triton's body, a scream erupted from the dead man's mouth as the Daemon, Vepar, was weakened by her own name.

"Where do you plan to go, Vepar? Another weak-minded one such as Triton?" The Daemon struggled as Lucien held it captive in the body of his former master. "Where o where shall you go, Vepar?" Lucien taunted. "You are weak and cannot go far, and you can only survive in this body for another ... what, quarter hour? Perhaps even less."

What are you doing?!

Lucien ignored the voice in his head as he continued watching the moving tattoo. "I'm afraid I cannot allow you to join with another. You see, as long as there are other Magi, I will not have complete power."

You're trying to kill her ... but you can't, please, let her go!

54

"However … you can join me. Bind with me and share your power with me."

It cannot be done!

"Silence, Zoran!" Lucien spat. "I know it can be done because you know it is possible."

The voice fell silent.

"Well?"

The tattoo on Triton's head ceased to move, and Lucien sighed heavily. "Oh, Vepar. You took too long." Lucien got to his feet, laying his former master's body on the ground as he heard footsteps racing toward him.

"Murderer! You will pay for this treachery!"

Lucien chuckled darkly as he glanced over his shoulder at the four Magi approaching him. "Will I?"

The sun began to set, and the Daemon Zoran was forced to watch as his great power destroyed the remaining leaders of the Magi.

And by the time the sun rose again and spread the light of dawn over the land, Lucien's swift rise to power was complete.

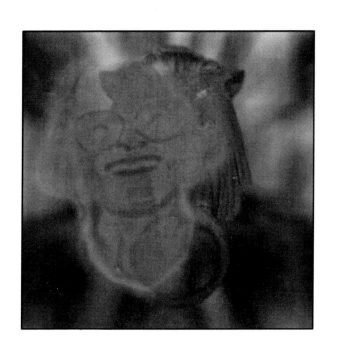

"Can't Hold a Candle To ... "
By
Sally Jean Genter

We drive our lives in quest of dreams; in turn, our dreams stem from events in our daily lives. In our unconscious world at night, they take form and shape us. But which dreams emerge to claim our devotion? How do we choose or compare?

"Can't Hold a Candle To ... " is a story of dreams. In a Dickens-like tale, perfect for a wintry night's reading session, we visit three of Francine Dennison's visions.

Each muse sprung from an aspect of my personal life. The recent loss of my own mother played out in Francine's fear of losing her grandmother. Her first dream found inspiration from a history book I read on a Roman emperor's daughter. The second dream, which I refer to as "Terror Under the Banyan," voices the cries that reached my ears from the persecuted, currently seeking refuge in the forests of Orissa, India.

"Can't hold a candle to ... " is an old saying. It takes a good thing and compares it to something better. You will have to decide for yourself what that key is. But in that process, be warned: some of Francine's nightmares may find their way into your consciousness.

⚷

"Can't hold a candle to hard work," Francine Dennison often quoted her grandmother's maxim. Well, it was almost her grandmother's saying. Grandma's words would be "Can't hold a candle to charity" or some other outmoded comparison. But Francine liked her adaptation; it reflected her drive to get ahead.

Securing an advantage over the next person was the key, through a dedicated, well-managed week. Six days at the office, four evenings at the gym, plenty of late-night hours researching articles to line up for the magazine, and one day set aside for chores – shopping, cleaning, and, if she had time, an occasional visit to see her family. That was her idea of the perfect week.

Habitually, the five-foot-seven twenty-six-year-old arrived back at her small but comfortable apartment in the city well after dark. Today was no exception. Closing the door, she tossed her keys on the Montello console table in the entryway and scooped up the mail from under the mail slot.

"Hmm." She shuffled through the stack. "Bills and a slew of holiday ads ... " She paused when her eyes caught on the red-and-green holly garland edging one store mailer. *Jesus, the reason for the season*, the holiday captioning read.

"Right," she lilted and rolled her eyes. "Why not be honest and say what you really mean: 'Money is the reason for the season.'" The short-haired blonde discarded the pile on the table near her keys.

It was that time of year again. In four short days the holiday shopping madness would begin. The thought made Francine shudder, sensing her well-oiled machine about to be knocked out of alignment for a few nostalgic moments under a badly trimmed tree.

"Bah humbug," she protested.

Chopin suddenly blared from her cell phone. Francine checked the Caller ID and answered, "Hi, sis."

"Hey, Francie," the voice on the other end said. "When do you plan to be here for Christmas? I'm trying to make plans for the family."

Francine's palm went to her forehead. "Oh, yeah, Christmas."

"You're coming, aren't you?" her sister quizzed.

"Work. It's been really busy lately."

"You're such a Scrooge," her sister sassed. "Well, when you decide if you're coming or not, call. Ciao, Ebenezer."

60

"Ha ha, very funny," Francine responded and ended the call.

Annoyed at Kristy's call, she entered the kitchen and pulled out a prepackaged salad from the fridge. "Not exactly gourmet, but it's healthy," she commented. Emptying the contents of the package in a bowl, she entertained ideas of avoiding the holiday rush.

Maybe buying online would spare the hassle of wasted time at the mall. Packages could be wrapped by merchants; they did that sort of thing for a few extra bucks. Token gifts, complete with ribbons and fluffy-worded note cards, could be mailed directly to her grandmother's house in lieu of her taking them there in person. Kristy and Mark, her siblings, would get over her not being home for the three-day weekend. It was her mother and grandmother she'd have difficultly explaining it to. But then, work always held up as a valid excuse, right?

Francine cringed. "You *are* a Scrooge," she echoed her sister's sentiment, this time laughing off the horridness of it. But all through the evening, Kristy's accusation would not leave her alone.

After hours of dodging the issue, bedtime, and the opportunity to escape her torment, finally came. To her room she trudged. Exhausted, the career woman clicked on the lamp next to her bed, and immediately did a double-take.

"Grandma?!" Her heart skipped a beat. From the corner of her eye, she thought she had seen her grandmother's face. But where she had imagined the likeness of the older woman, Scrooge's lion-faced doorknocker grinned up at her from the cover of a book.

"What are you smirking at?" she scolded, as if it could hear her. In one contemptuous movement, she turned the book face down to silence any imagined response.

Shrugging it off, she plumped her pillow against her headboard, climbed in, and pulled the covers up to her chest.

"Ah, which book shall I bore myself to sleep with tonight?" she mused. The selection on her nightstand

61

consisted of the Dickens book she had just hallucinated her grandmother's face on, a historical novel her sister had given her, and her grandmother's book of Psalms. Not wanting to fill her pre-bedtime thoughts with more Christmas or her grandmother, she pulled *Most Noble Girl* from the middle of the stack and turned to the first page.

Galla Placidia, the almost Empress of Rome, it began. Hours later, Francine found she could not put the book down. The fabricated biography told of a Roman emperor's daughter many thought destined to be an empress. But through a series of events – sparked with pageantry, tyranny, and betrayal – the princess wound up exiled. Tragically, her remains burned to ashes by a schoolchild's wayward taper some 1,100 years after her death.

Nearly finished with the novel, Francine Dennison's eyelids felt like lead and finally she could keep them open no longer. Placidia's mysterious betrayal of her loyal cousin, Serena, was the diverted reader's last reflection before she nodded off to sleep.

⊖━┳

Francine woke to a burning sensation. Her flesh was on fire.

"Ouch!" she yelped and jerked her hand from the heat source. The sudden movement caused a heavy, multi-branched candelabrum to waver in her other fist. Before it could topple, she grabbed it with her singed palm to steady it.

"Placidia," a female's voice intruded. "We must speak."

Disoriented, Francine lifted her eyes to see a stately, but kind-looking woman walking hastily in her direction. She wore a strange gown of white pleated linen, pinned at the shoulder with a gold medallion.

"E-excuse me?" Francine stammered.

"Placidia, listen carefully. I do not know how much time we have."

Placidia? Francine looked around to see no one but her in the room. And the room … nothing in it rang with familiarity. Large white columns abutted the structure, each pillar draped in colorful linen like the woman wore. Francine caught a glimpse of her own reflection in a mirror. She too had on the loose-fitting linen robe, only hers glimmered profusely with gold thread and ribbons. Then she realized: The face in the reflection did not belong to her. Instead, it belonged to a girl several years her junior who stared back at her with a dropped jaw.

"My dear cousin," the woman interjected again, this time with more command, "you'll burn yourself, and all of Rome, the way you're holding that candelabrum." She reached out and corrected the younger woman's grip on the stem as though she were accustomed to instructing her. She continued, "Rumor circulates that Alaric marches on Rome and that the Senate looks for a scapegoat to blame. With my late Stilicho's fall from favor, I fear they'll pin the conspiracy on me."

"Serena!" Francine exclaimed, beginning to grasp what transpired. It smacked of a chapter right out of her book. "Your husband, Stilicho, was murdered," she revealed from memory.

"Bite your tongue, Placidia," the woman snapped. "Take care what you speak within these walls. If the Senate were to hear you, they would doubt your loyalty to Rome."

"But I speak truth," she defended. The growing familiarly of her assumed role fueled her confidence. "Stilicho may have been a barbarian, but he did nothing scandalous, save annoy the wrong person. And you are no conspirator; you should defend yourself."

Serena smiled and gently held Francine's cheek. "My dear cousin, this is why you must promise that you will let me go."

"Go?"

"Yes, go," Serena confirmed. "I have mentored you, and you have worked hard. Someday you will be empress."

63

"Empress?" Francine's countenance wavered. She knew the story. Galla Placidia would never be empress, though she tried.

"I will not let you throw away your career on my account," Serena insisted. She took her cousin firmly by the shoulders. "When they come for me, you must stand with them."

"Betray you." Her words fell flat. As silence passed between them, Francine became acutely aware of the rising smoke from the tallow candelabrum tapers she held. It possessed the eerie quality of Serena's life diffusing by her hand – a wrong Placidia could never blot from her record. The thought struck her, that if she refused to betray her cousin, maybe she could change Placidia's fate, too. But as the idea took shape, the door opened, sending a draft in to frustrate the flames and scatter the smoke.

In stepped a Roman soldier – spear in hand and clad in armor. His stone face swiveled in Serena's direction. "On charges of conspiracy, you are sentenced to be strangled until dead." His proclamation echoed off the walls like a boulder ricocheting down a bottomless well.

Nothing could have prepared Francine for what happened next.

"*Arrrrrrh!*" Serena wailed and clutched her face.

Placidia's wannabe came undone. *No! This cannot happen,* she wanted to shout. *The Senate lies,* she screamed inwardly. But outwardly she said nothing, only stared, transfixed and unable to move. Francine felt she acted out the pages of a novel rather than of her own free will.

In the melee, she had not noticed the taper flame wandering too closely to her royal garb.

"Placidia," the soldier's voice broke her trance.

She looked to see his stone eyes fixated on her and felt fear.

"Your gown has caught fire." He delivered the news without warmth, in the same manner he had Serena's death sentence.

As if on cue, her gold-embroidered sleeve ignited into flames. "Oh!" Francine gasped. She jerked the candelabra away from her garment, but the fire continued to consume her.

The soldier strode across the marble floor to extinguish the blaze in his large, fleshy palms. His eyes met her frantic ones and she paled. Something about his calm gave her the creeps.

"What's your cousin's life to you?" he grated. "You can't hold a candle to being empress, can you?" His mocking words preceded a low, rumbling laughter that grew into a full-bellowed roar.

Stunned, Francine pulled away from him — the candelabra still in her grip.

"Stop!" she cried. But he would not. His laughter echoed louder and louder, until it pierced her soul. Without strength, she stumbled backward and collapsed. Down, into a bottomless void she tumbled. Her dream world snuffed out, except for the taper flames that flickered to the soldier's haunting laughter.

⚸

A tumult of bedcovers rose from where Francine slept. From underneath them, a terror-shaken woman bolted upright. Her hair jutted in all directions and her eyes blazed wildly. It took a few dozen heartbeats to ground herself on the familiar walls and furniture of her own bedroom. At last, she let out a deep sigh of relief.

To reaffirm her reality, she tossed the covers aside. Her hands shook noticeably.

"Calm down," she berated herself and proceeded to abandon her bed. As she did, a lump slid from the comforter.

Thud.

Still in a daze, she looked down to see the novel on Galla Placidia by her feet. Francine stooped over to pick it up, and reflectively placed it on the nightstand.

65

"See, it was just a dream," she placated her imagination. A much calmer hand ran through her moppy hair, and she dismissed the unsettled feeling.

She meandered to the kitchen and filled a glass with ice water. Its coolness felt good trickling down her throat. Much relieved, she picked up the newspaper from the counter and leafed through to the crossword puzzle.

"Aha, just the mindless activity I need to get my brain off Rome and lull me back to sleep." She tucked the paper under her arm and headed for bed again.

Climbing under the covers, she propped herself up against the headboard and slapped the paper open in her lap. "Hmm, let's see, a word for *Indian fig tree* ... Banyan!" Her slender fingers penciled the letters in the blocks and read the next clue. Before she knew it, her pencil and newspaper slipped from her hands and her head slumped to the pillow.

⊶

Francine heard whispers and muffled sobs. She opened her eyes, or at least she thought she had, because she could see almost nothing. It was dark and it felt as though she were outside. There was a crick in her neck, like she'd been in an uncomfortable position for hours. Squinting, she made out faint shapes of vine-like tree branches and shadows of faces, but still had no idea where she was or who the silhouettes were.

"Esther," a female's voice gently called.

The accented whisper came from a twentyish woman with short brown hair. She looked vaguely familiar, but Francine couldn't place from where. Feeling a slight déjà vu connection with her previous dream of being a Roman princess, she looked for telltale signs of her setting. But the place they crouched in and the woman waiting for her to answer looked destitute instead of royal.

She put her fingertips to her chest. "Me … Esther?" she finally croaked. Her throat felt rough, as though she hadn't spoken in some time. She also sounded young, at best a teen.

"Poor dear, no child should have to experience this trauma," the stranger said compassionately. "Come." She patted a spot by her side with one hand and extended a fruit of some sort with the other. "Eat. It's not the tastiest, but you'll feel better with something in your stomach."

Francine took the fruit in her small hand and examined it. It looked to be some sort of fig. As a kid, she'd eaten plenty of figs grown at her grandparents' farmhouse. She bit into the flesh and made a face. "Eww, yuck!" she rasped, and immediately spewed it out. It tasted bitter and the texture felt gritty.

Looking at the fruit, she felt nauseated. There, nestled in its flesh rested half of whatever insect had burrowed into it. "There's … a bug in it," she managed to choke out.

"Shh," the woman hushed. "We mustn't let our voices be heard." She pulled Francine nearer and held her in her arms. "I'm sorry about the fig wasp. I didn't know it was there." She smiled contagiously.

Francine immediately forgot the insect and smiled back. "I forgive you," she said. Something about this angelic woman comforted her. She hadn't felt the security of another person in a long time. It reminded her of evenings curled up with mother on the sofa, sharing girl talk and giggles.

"Perhaps God wanted to remind us that He works miracles in mysterious ways," she said.

The puzzled response on Francine's face must have been obvious, because the woman went on to explain.

"Sure. Think about it. In these forests grow the largest trees in the world, banyans," she reasoned. "In God's foresight, He knew that tonight we would find shelter in one of them. So He began his miracle with a small fruit, like the one you bit into."

Francine scrunched her nose at the unpleasant reminder.

The storyteller chuckled softly and continued. "Esther, it took more than a lone fruit to give birth to this tree. God can create anything instantly, but sometimes does His greater works when His creations work together. God entrusted the tiny fig wasp with the important task of pollinating the banyan tree. It does so by burrowing into the fruit, mating, and leaving one to die inside. But while baby wasps are produced from that death, the greater miracle of a new banyan is born in the process. Tonight we're sitting in a tree that God planned more than 100 years ago through the obedience of a tiny part of His creation."

"That's God's miracle?" Francine asked. She wasn't convinced she saw their predicament in the same light. But at least she gleaned what they were doing there – hiding. But from who?

"Sure," the angelic-like woman answered. She pulled Francine closer. "God does not always work in blaring ways, but His works are big all the same. If I didn't believe that, I wouldn't be here as a missionary."

Missionary. Now Francine had a key piece of the puzzle. If her companion was a missionary, it would explain why she watched over her the way she did. While her questions raged, one thing she knew: their predicament felt real. She looked at the half-bitten-into fruit and her stomach rumbled. Not only did she hunger, she began to feel cold, tired, and afraid.

As if on cue, their solitude dissipated by the intrusion of angry shouts filling the night. A volley of hushed whispers rose from others under the banyan, and then they fell silent, leaving only the sound of approaching rioters on the air.

"The villagers found us," the missionary whispered tensely. She looked at Francine and squeezed her small frame reassuringly. "Esther, whatever happens, I want you to know you are special and that God loves you. Stick close to me and I promise to watch over you. If we need to run, run as fast as you can and don't let go." With that she took Francine's hand and peered out from their nook in the tree.

Francine tugged at her hand, feeling impatient. The longer they stood there, the more afraid she felt. Overwhelming fear of death pricked at her. Intimidating torch flames grew nearer, dancing tauntingly against the blackness. Panicked, she could wait no longer and bolted from the missionary's side.

Several angry villagers saw her darting from the cover of the banyan. "Over there!" they cried and changed their direction. Encroaching flames circled the tree; they bobbed up and down to the shouts.

Francine froze, shocked. She wanted to take her action back, but it was too late. Suddenly, a cry of terror arose from under the banyan like none she'd ever heard before. Out of nowhere, hundreds of people – men, women, and children – emerged from hiding. All of them fled from the approaching mob in a panic. Francine instantly lost her bearing in the tumult.

Their cover was blown and all because of her. Francine felt the pelting of human bodies jostling her as they ran past. Instead of joining them, she looked back to find the face of the missionary. A small break in the crowd revealed her in the clutches of an angry man with a torch.

The missionary saw her too. "Run!" she let out a bloodcurdling scream.

But Francine could only stand there and watch.

The grinning man saw her and looked through to her soul. "Don't worry about the others," he taunted. "Can't hold a candle to saving yourself." His words chilled her to the bone. And like the man from her previous dream, he began to laugh maliciously while wrestling with the young missionary woman in his clutches.

⌐—

Francine shot up in bed for the second time that night. She pulled her body into a fetal position and clung to the bedcovers, whimpering uncontrollably.

Why was she having these nightmares?

Her eyes fell to the newspaper beside her on her bed. A picture of a large banyan tree, just like the one from her dream, took up a portion of the front page. In disbelief, she picked the paper up to have a closer look. From under the tree the kindly face of the missionary smiled up at her.

"That can't be," she gaped. Skimming the article, it explained that the woman worked in a nearby orphanage and died while trying to get children away from rioters.

"You were so real," she whispered. Then her expression dropped, realizing she'd dreamt about a dead woman. Angry, she threw the paper down. She didn't want to think about it anymore. Climbing out of bed, she knew she'd never fall back to sleep now.

Francine strolled to her kitchen again. This time she noticed the light on her recorder blinking and she remembered she hadn't checked for messages earlier. She pushed the button and listened.

"Hi, Fran," her grandmother's fragile voice said. "I'm sorry I missed you. I miss hearing your voice. I'm looking forward to seeing you for Christmas. I love you."

The message ended. And Francine groaned. "Ugh, Christmas." She had to work; she didn't have time for that silly gathering. She looked at the clock on the stove. Still too early; she'd have to call her later. Francine grabbed a pen from the counter to write a note for the refrigerator: Call Grandma in the morning to cancel Christmas.

Deciding not to return to bed, she went into the living room and clicked on the TV. "The cooking channel sounds harmless," she remarked. Nestling into her sofa, she watched how to prepare Cornish game hen. Somewhere between selecting the right bird and spicing it to perfection, she fell asleep.

"Didn't forget the thyme, did you?" Grandma's old, but familiar voice chimed.

For a split second Francine had no idea where she was. With a head of lettuce in one hand and a half-unpacked grocery bag in the other, her mind filled in her whereabouts as being Grandma's kitchen. But not everything was quite right; this was more like a dream.

"What did you say?" she faced her grandmother to ask.

"The thyme. You did get the thyme, didn't you?" the older woman repeated.

Francine nearly gasped at the aged look of her grandmother. Had it been that long? She began to calculate … four, no, nine months ago since Christmas. Before that, she stopped having dinners at Grandma's the year she had moved to the city. Still, this didn't seem right; she couldn't be as old as she looked.

"Are you going to stand there and make an old woman wait or are you going to answer me?" her grandmother prodded.

"Oh!" Francine snapped out of her stare. She dug into the grocery bag and rummaged around. "Sorry, I guess I forgot the thyme," she relayed.

Her grandmother's sweet laugh filled the kitchen. "Fran, you never could remember. It's a good thing I have some in the garden. Old man Grimble came by in the spring and planted it for me. He knows how much I love to cook with it. Personally, I think he's hoping I'll make some Cornish hen for him now that it's ripened." She laughed again. "Why don't you go and pick some while I set the table, dear."

Now Francine knew this wasn't right. Mr. Grimble no longer lived nearby. But with Grandma's high spirits, how could Francine refuse? She pressed open the back door screen and stepped out on the large plantation-style porch. Nothing

71

but a lone rocker sat on the aging wooden platform now; Papa's had been gone for years.

Grandma lived alone in that big farmhouse. How many times had Mom and her siblings tried to pry Grandma away from it, but to no avail. Moving would be like amputating her right arm. She loved that place, along with all its memories.

Tonight's dinner was proof of that. Cornish game hen was grandma's "Friday night special," as Papa used to say. And Grandma always made sure it tasted perfect. Thyme, fresh from her garden, was her secret ingredient. But as many times as she'd say it, Francine would always seem to forget. She guessed she just had more important things on her mind, like … well she couldn't think of any at the moment, but they were more important than cooking hens.

Francine carefully selected a batch of thyme, which conveniently grew in abundance in this dream garden. She rubbed a small sprig of it between her fingers and put it up to her nose. *Mmm.* It smelled authentic. Satisfied she'd collected enough of the spice, she returned to the house.

Inside, she watched her grandmother carefully remove the hen from the side-by-side refrigerator. This time, she only removed one. In the past, Francine recalled her taking four or five out from the old Kenmore. And when company filed in – old man Grimble or other neighbors from down the lane – she'd have to make a second trip for more. But everyone knew what to expect – Friday night's menu was Cornish hen.

Tonight, she moved slowly, like she was old and tired. Eighty-six and two knee surgeries later, she'd had a full life. At least Francine guessed that was her age; this dream made her grandmother look so much older. Regardless, her days for moving fast had past. Lord only knew if the whole clan had been there, she'd never have been able to keep up with them all.

But they weren't all there, only grandmother and granddaughter … and Francine's cell phone that wouldn't stop ringing. Each time Chopin played from the electronic device, it solicited the habitual maneuver for the holster on her hip. First it was Ben, then Ashleigh, and after that a train of others. It never stopped.

"Fran, remember the time," Grandma started … and the blasted phone rang again.

The final time, Francine checked her Caller ID, and answered, "Julie, you caught me at a bad time. I won't be able to get those files to you until morning."

The voice on the other side of the phone explained she couldn't wait. Late was fine, but she needed them tonight.

Francine sighed. "Tonight then," she submitted and disconnected the call.

"Grandma," Francine said and rose from the dinning room table, "I really have to get going."

Her grandmother didn't say a thing, just slowly stood and gave her a kiss before she left.

Francine could say she hadn't noticed, but a quaint thought in the recesses of her mind told her she'd forgotten something, something important. But the eluding thought got lost on the blurry drive home. And it remained lost through the motions of doing work late into the night.

Finally, she met Julie's deadline and retired to bed. But sleep felt non-existent. Before she knew it, Francine's phone roused her.

Kristy, her sister, called to inform her that Grandma had been readying for bed after Francine had left and felt her chest tighten. Somehow, she'd managed to dial 911 on her old rotary phone. But by the time the ambulance arrived, she'd already passed.

Without words, Francine hung up her phone.

Time got away from her before the cell rang again. This time she saw her boss's number on the display.

"Julie," she answered. The clock on the microwave read 9:11 a.m. Work! She palmed her forehead. "I apologize profusely for being late. My grandmother passed away."

"I'm so sorry, Francie. Don't worry about work … can't hold a candle to thyme," Francine thought she heard her say.

"Thyme?" Francine piqued. "What did you say?"

"I said, I'm out of time," her boss repeated. Her tinny laugh projected from the earpiece before the connection severed.

Francine stared at the phone, trying to sort out what she'd just heard. Julie's laughter struck her as hollow, unthoughtful, even sardonic. It left Francine feeling numb, like she'd just been slapped in the face.

⚬⊥

Dawn broke and Francine stirred. Slumped over on the sofa, she still had the remote in her hand. A commercial for a cooking show droned on in the background. She clicked the TV off and raised a palm to her forehead. "Ugh," she moaned. "What an awful night of dreams."

Dreams was right … all vivid and disturbing. She'd watched a lovely woman go to her death while she stood by and said nothing. Serena had been gone for nearly two millennia. But as silly as it sounded, Francine felt as though she'd lost someone dear. She also felt she'd witnessed the death of Galla Placidia's innocence. Whether out of obedience to her cousin or outright betrayal, the misguided death of Placidia's mentor may have cost her the title of empress.

On the other hand, the night of terror under the banyan had only taken place a few days ago, according to the newspaper. The picture of the missionary squatting next to a little girl no more than eleven years of age would stick with her a long time. She'd always remember the sweet voice of the angel who'd shared God's love for her through the miraculous death of a fig wasp. Francine felt compelled to call the young woman's family to tell them what a brave and wonderfully unselfish person she had been.

It made Francine think of her own family. The dream about Grandma was fresh. She felt ashamed. What had she done with her life except watch out for number one, herself? Would anyone remember her fondly after she died? Francine

74

looked around at her small apartment. The sum of her legacy … stuff.

"Can't hold a candle to charity," she heard her grandmother's sweet voice. Charity. Francine wrote for a living; she knew the definition of the word. "Any generous act to aid another, motivated by sincere kindness and love; a God-given quality," she recited from memory. Her grandmother often said there was no greater example of charity than God the Father giving his Son on Christmas day.

Christmas!

"Grandma!" Her eyes flew open and she jumped to her feet. "It may be too late for Serena and that missionary, but I hope it's not too late for Grandma." Francine's heart quickened. What if her grandmother had died last night? It was only six in the morning, but she had to know. Francine left her living room on a mission to find her cell phone.

Ironically, it sat on her nightstand, atop the stack of books.

"That's odd," she said and picked it up; she didn't remember leaving it there. Leaning against the edge of her bed, she selected her grandmother's number and waited. After a few rings she heard the familiar voice on the other side of the phone and relaxed.

"Hello," the sweet elderly voice answered.

"Hi, Grandma."

"Fran, is that you?"

"Yes, it's me."

"It's still rather early. Is everything all right?"

"Yes. Everything's fine." The truth was, now that she knew her grandmother was all right, everything was fine.

Francine's eyes fell to where her phone had been. There was Dickens' book with the illustration of Ebenezer Scrooge's doorknocker on its cover. She recalled her night of dreams and a corner of her mouth quirked upward.

"Grandma, I'm convinced that God doesn't always work in blaring ways, but His works are big all the same."

The elderly woman's soft voice chuckled. "Yes, I believe He does, Fran. That's a good saying, too. Wish I'd thought of it."

"Grandma, if I recall, you've got a pretty good one yourself." She recited her grandmother's maxim: "Can't hold a candle to charity."

Her grandmother was right; Francine had it all wrong. The key wasn't about working hard to get ahead; it was about taking care of others. She'd been so focused on herself that she'd lost sight of the more important things, like the relationships that were dear to her. She didn't want her own life to end up like the ones in her dreams. A change had to be made, and it would start now.

"Grandma, I just wanted to call and tell you I'm looking forward to seeing you at Christmas."

Her grandmother's sweet laughter filled her ears. "You can't hold a candle to a beautiful granddaughter," she said. "Good-bye, dear."

"Bye, Grandma," Francine replied and pressed the button to end the call. She smiled at her grandmother's new use of her phrase. It felt good, knowing she was bringing joy into a very special lady's life.

Francine believed she'd found the key to success.

⚷

"If"
By
Chris Whigham

Is a man defined by what he has, or who he is? Stanley is going to find the answer to that question very shortly as he is confronted by his past, and questions his future.

⚍—⊤

"I take care of the old fart for three months while he's in a coma, and all I get is a friggin' key!" Stanley Winkelman was furious. So furious, in fact, that he could barely keep his '79 Oldsmobile on the dark road.

His wife, Gloria, had never seen him like this. He had been screaming like a lunatic since they left the attorney's office. It was time for her to use all of the womanly wiles and charm she possessed to help calm him down.

"Stanley, will you shut the hell up and pay attention to the road?! You're gonna get us both killed!" That was all of the charm she could muster for the moment.

He pounded his foot on the brake, and the old behemoth slid off the country road, skidding to a stop in the gravel. Stanley's knuckles were white from grasping the steering wheel. Half fear of the skid, half anger from the night's events. He turned to Gloria, whose hair was partially out of its clip and dangling in her face. She had a death-grip on the dashboard.

"You have got to calm down." She took a deep breath and leaned back in her seat.

Obviously in no mood to take advice from someone not as incensed as he was, Stanley exited the car and slammed the door shut. He made it about twenty feet down the road before he slumped against a tree.

Gloria sighed, and followed suit. She loved her husband, but never knew any man that could be as emotional as he could be. Aren't security guards supposed to be level-headed?

"Stanley," she started. "So what? So what if Uncle Jonas only left us a key? Frankly, we're lucky he left us anything."

"Lucky? He was a crazy, delusional nut job! He spent the last ten years of his life locked in that dungeon he called a basement, doing Lord knows what, ranting like a madman about the choices he made … and I was the only one who ever gave a damn about him."

She leaned into him for a comforting hug, something she was very good at.

"And he gave all of it to that cat!" He stood up and walked away, causing Gloria to lose her balance and hit the ground.

"It's the friggin' lottery all over again!" One night, several years back, Stanley made the decision to finish watching a football game instead of buying a lottery ticket. His usual numbers were picked, and three million dollars slipped through his fingers.

He'd never been able to enjoy football again.

"One point six million … to a cat!" His voice trembled with rage. "For three months, I fed that … that … " He turned around and spotted his wife on the ground.

"Gloria! I'm having a major crisis here and you're lounging around?"

She stood up, brushing crud off of her pantsuit. She was glad she chose the earth-tone design for tonight's will reading. Although, when the evening began, she had no idea she would end up rolling around in the dirt on County Road 29.

"Stanley, think about it. Uncle Jonas was lonely. That cat has been his only friend for the past 11 years. And, let's be honest … we haven't been much of a family to him."

He took a deep breath. Then another one. He hated when she used logic to diffuse an argument. He had no way to fight it.

"I know. I know. It's just that … well, I thought that if I was there for him at the end, he might … "

"He might give it all to us?" She finished his sentences frequently, much to his distaste. "Stanley, really now. Didn't you spend these last months with him and … Mr. Paws … out of love?"

He thought for a moment. "Well, not love, so much as guilt. You're right. After Aunt Lilly died, we were all he had, and we treated him like the black sheep. The crazy, delusional black sheep."

Gloria put her arms around him and hugged him. He hugged back, and felt a calm come over himself.

"It's just that, for once, I thought we could get ahead. I have been so sick and tired of being a minimum wage rent-a-cop at a third-rate drug store, driving a 30-year-old car, who can't pay his bills and can barely take care of his family." A tear escaped his left eye.

She held on tight. For all the stress and trouble they'd been through lately, they were all each other had.

⊶

At two in the morning, the pill was just as hard to swallow. Dead uncle, no inheritance.

"Ah," Stanley said, quietly to himself, "he did leave me something."

He held an awkwardly large key up to the dim kitchen light. It was as long as his hand, and constructed out of a thin metal, like tin. It was very crude, as well, almost like it had been cut with a hand-saw.

"What in the world could this possibly fit?" *Nothing of value* was his first thought.

There was an envelope that came with the key, and now was as good a time as any to open it. The attorney indicated it was a personal letter from Jonas, to be opened in private.

The envelope was of poor quality. The man was a millionaire, and he still bought his stationery at a dime store. Stanley imagined having his Uncle's money … his stationery would be monogrammed, probably imported from Spain. Or China. Or wherever the really good paper came from.

The cheap glue gave way easily, and revealed the contents of the envelope … a piece of notebook paper, which had been carelessly ripped from its housing. Though harmless, the jagged edges aggravated Stanley even more.

As he unfolded the note, he noticed his uncle had used his favorite writing utensil … a red marker. That damned marker. When he was a kid, spending his summers with his uncle and aunt, Jonas would make him write reports on his daily activities. Then, as if deriving a sadistic pleasure from tormenting the youth, would correct it in red marker.

That damned marker.

The light was almost too dim to read, but a 40-watt bulb was all he had until payday, so it would have to do. He slid his coffee mug aside, and leaned over the letter to get a good, close look.

Stanley,
If you're reading this, then the bad news is I'm dead. But the good news is, I've found a way to come back from the dead, and I'm standing behind you right now!

Stanley refused to give into the final musings of a dead nut job. Although … no, he wouldn't look.

Seriously … Stanley, you probably know by now that I've left my fortune to Mr. Paws. And, knowing you, that knowledge does not make you happy.

And this letter isn't helping. His hands began to tremble with anger, making it a little harder to read.

*Don't blame Mr. Paws. He's just a cat. But I need you to
know something, Stanley. You were the only family I had.
And we may not have seemed close in my final years, but
you were always in my thoughts. You, and Lilly. Stanley, I
miss her so much. I should have been there that day ...
with her, in the car.*

Jonas had always blamed himself for Aunt Lilly's death.
He was busy working when she had a doctor's appointment,
so she went by herself. She never saw the black ice on the turn
...

*The key I left you is worth more than any amount of
money I had. You'll see, Stanley. That key will help you
see things. Things the way they could have been. Just
remember this ... life is only about the choices you've
made. So choose well, Stanley. Choose well.*

Choose well? Choose what well?

P.S. Mr. Paws just ate a bird. He's such a good kitty!

"I hate that cat," Stanley mumbled.
And that was the last thought he had before he fell asleep
at the kitchen table.

⌐—🗝

Morning came early, and the drive to Jonas' house was a
long one. Since he was the last of the living relatives, it was
up to Stanley to pack up the old coot's stuff. Six decades of
stuff, to be exact. It would take days to go through everything,
and would cost him some vacation time. But that was okay; he
couldn't afford to go anywhere anyway.
    The drive would take about two hours, but that was okay.
It gave him time to remember. To remember some of those

summers he spent at the old country home. Jonas was a taskmaster who demanded perfection out of young Stanley, but Aunt Lilly balanced him out with home-cooked meals, long walks in the woods, and bedtime stories about lands far away.

Those were good memories, and now it seemed to be a land far, far away that he could never return to. Simpler times, when his life was full of promise, instead of regret.

A shiver crept down his spine as he rounded the corner where Lilly spent her last living moments. In the morning light, it was hard to believe that something as simplistic as ice took her life.

You never know, he thought.

With memories flooding his mind, the final miles went quickly, and he was at the driveway before he knew it. The quarter-mile gravel path to the house rattled his car, reminding him that he drove a piece of junk.

As the house came into view, Stanley laughed to himself. For a man that had more money than he, or now his cat, knew what to do with, he sure didn't mind living in a veritable shack. Even to a guy who was penniless, this house seemed like a dump!

The Olds squealed to a stop, and he exited, reluctantly. He stared at the front door for a long moment, and sighed. This was a task that he was not looking forward to.

Stanley walked up the warped front stairs. On the third step, he stopped, as he felt the wood beneath his foot crack under the weight. He skipped it, and stretched up to the fourth step, and made his way to the door.

He dug in his pocket for the house keys, and opened the screen door. Not surprisingly, it only opened half way. Like everything else in the old place, it was broken.

Stepping through the door was like stepping into a museum. The living area of the house had been virtually untouched since his aunt died. Jonas had set up his basement/workshop with everything he needed to live. There was a cot, an old refrigerator and hot plate, and even a rudimentary toilet.

Stanley hadn't been down there since Lilly's funeral. He had to coax his uncle away from his work and into a suit presentable enough for the service. It was as if he was in denial.

And from that day forward, Jonas was driven to complete his work. He worked through holidays, dinner invites, and birthdays. He even skipped visiting the cemetery on the anniversary of Lilly's death … as if it wasn't a permanent thing.

The only person Jonas ever allowed in the basement was his neighbor Earl. Earl was a retired professor from MIT, and they had played chess against each other for years. But after the funeral, their relationship seemed more … serious. In fact, it was Earl that discovered the comatose body.

Well, the basement was as good a place to start as any.

He stepped carefully through the living room, trying to navigate around the antique furniture. Unfortunately, he couldn't avoid stepping on Mr. Paw's tail.

The fat orange feline screeched, and scrambled into the kitchen. Surprised, Stanley tumbled into the buffet and broke a collectable plate depicting the moon landing.

"I hate that stupid cat," he mumbled. "That stupid, rich cat."

He righted himself, and made his way to the basement door. He stopped and stared at it for a while. This was his uncle's inner sanctum, his personal space. It almost felt like a violation to enter.

But then he thought about getting screwed in the will, and the hesitation vanished.

The door squeaked open, and Stanley flipped the light switch. Nothing. *Damn! Doesn't anything in this house work?*

He shrugged, and carefully walked down the steps. It was one of those narrow stairwells that are common in old houses. He had never been claustrophobic, but this was probably as close as it got.

At the bottom, he fumbled along the wall for another light switch. It was dark … very dark. And he didn't like touching things he couldn't see. The wall was cool, and the bricks were jagged. His hand brushed through webs and loose grout and … was that something squishy?

Finally, he found the switch. A series of fluorescent lights began to flicker on across the room. What was revealed in the newfound brightness was nothing short of amazing!

Section by section, the project, or whatever it was, that his uncle had been working on, was brought into the open. The basement was twice as large as the house … Jonas must have had it enlarged at some point. Hundreds of yards of copper wiring and PVC tubing lined the walls and ceiling. Dozens of computers, all connected to each other, were stacked on a series of shelves.

Along one wall was a glass case with some sort of crystal collection encased. When the power came on, the colorful rocks began to glow, and … yes, and hum!

In the center of the room, a small desk and chair, like one that a student might use. On the desk was a black metal box, the size of a small television, with a screen on the front and a microphone attached to the top.

But what caught his attention was the thing connected to the contraption: a smaller box, with a red button and a … key slot.

Stanley reached in his shirt pocket, and pulled out the key that his uncle had left him. He held the cheap piece of molded tin up to the bad lighting, and it looked as unimpressive as ever. But, it had to be the key that fit into that slot.

He stepped toward the desk, and prepared to see what all of the secrecy was about. Could this have been what Jonas spent the last decade screwing around with? Would this explain what he meant by "different choices"?

He reached out with the key, lined it up with the slot and …

"Stanley!"

He jumped a foot in the air, startled by the voice behind him. The key flew out of his hand and dropped on the cement floor.

He turned and saw Earl, Jonas' friend. He was tall and distinguished, well into his sixties, and could still scare the bejesus out of Stanley!

"Earl! What the hell?!"

"Sorry, son!" The older man laughed heartily. "It's good to know I can still sneak up on someone."

Stanley picked up the key, and sat in the chair.

"What are you doing here?"

"I was out for my walk, and thought I saw your car here." Earl strolled around the room, gliding his hand along some of the tubes. "I really miss the old coot, Stanley."

"Yeah, so do I."

"He truly loved you. You were the son he never had."

"Really?" This surprised Stanley. And also brought on another bought of instant guilt. Jonas had rarely been in his thoughts.

"Yes," Earl continued. "Every time I was over here, he would talk you up. 'Stanley used to do this,' and 'Stanley would always do that.' He really loved those summers you spent here."

There was a moment of awkward silence. The hum from the crystal chamber was the only sound for what seemed like hours.

"Son, I know he left you the key. The key to that thing." Earl pointed to the black box.

"What is it, Earl? What does it do?"

"I'm not quite sure, Stanley. But I do know that since Lilly passed, it was the most important thing in his life. He spent twenty hours a day for the past ten years working on it, and it's where I found him ... slumped over the desk, in that coma."

They both stared at it, each curious about what it did.

"Stanley, he wanted you to use it. That's why he gave you the key. But ... just be careful."

Earl turned, and began up the stairs.

"Thanks," Stanley added.

The old man looked back. "Son, just be careful. Remember what Jonas always said: it's about the choices we made."

And he was gone.

Stanley looked back at the desk, held up the key, and took a deep breath.

"Uncle Jonas, this is for you."

The key fit perfectly. Since it was fairly flimsy, he was careful when he turned it. There was a slight click, and it stopped turning. The red button lit up, and begged to be pushed.

He sat down, carefully. The crystals began to hum louder, and almost warned against what he was about to do. Sweat began to drip from his brow, and his hands became numb with anxiety. He hadn't been this nervous since his big foul shot at the end of the high school tournament game. The one he missed, which lost his school the championship.

Screw it!

His right hand rose in the air, paused, and came down on the glowing button. The lights flickered, the humming got louder, and the sweat increased. He closed his eyes, awaiting the fate that was about to pounce on him.

And ... nothing.

He opened his eyes and looked around. Everything looked normal. Lights, crystals, everything. Except the screen on the box was now illuminated.

A sentence appeared in bright green letters and a mechanical voice said:

"If only I would have ... "

"If only I would have?" he repeated. "If only I would have ... what?"

"If only I would have ... "

86

Now, this was curious. Was he supposed to answer?

"If only I would have ... "

And then it hit him. This is what Jonas meant about choices! The box wants him to play a "What if?" game!

"If only I would have ... "

"Okay," Stanley answered. "I'll play the game."

He thought for a moment, and smiled. The game ... the basketball game! He was branded a loser after that game, so why not play along and use that moment of his life?

"Okay ... if only I would have made the foul shot in the championship high school game."

The fluorescent lights went out, and there was a moment of deathly silence.

And then hell was unleashed.

The crystal chamber exploded in light. The shelves of computers came to life, and there was a sound like a jackhammer from behind the walls.

That was the last thing Stanley remembered as he blacked out.

⊶

"C'mon, Stan the Man! You can do it!"

Stan opened his eyes. The roar of the crowd was deafening. He looked around, and a thousand fans were rooting for him to make the basket.

He looked up at the scoreboard. Zero seconds left on the clock, and they were down by one. His buddy, Jerry, stood at the baseline and cheered him on.

"You can do it, Stan!"

The basket seemed a mile away, but that was okay. He had practiced this shot hundreds of times, and was ready.

He bounced the ball three times, bent his knees, and took aim. The ball flew from his hands as if someone else was in control.

And *swoosh*. Nothing but net!

The crowd went nuts! Jerry ran over and slapped his back.

"One more, Stan. One more!"

He bounced the ball three more times, and paused. Suddenly, he lost feeling in his hands. Sweat burned his eyes, and his vision blurred. But he let go of the ball anyway.

It was just like the movies. The ball floated through the air in slow motion, careening toward the basket. It bounced off the back part of the rim, straight up. On the way down, it glanced off the right side, swirled around the top, and dropped down the middle.

He did it! He made the shot! They won the championship!

The crowd came out of their seats, and rushed the court. Stan's teammates hefted him up on their shoulders and paraded him around the court. It was the greatest celebration he could have ever imagined ... and it was all for him. He was the hero!

Was that supposed to happen? Didn't he miss it ... the first time? What was happening?

It didn't matter. Right now, he was on top of the world.

"Stan!" It was a girl's voice. He looked down into the crowd, and saw Jenny Williams. The most beautiful girl he knew, shouting at him.

"Stan! Way to go! We're all going to a party tonight at Beth Inman's house! Go with me, okay?"

"Uh, sure." That was all he could get out. Not only was Beth Inman the most popular girl at school, but Jenny Williams would never have given him the time of day before, let alone be seen in public with him!

Stan went to the party that night, and started to hang out with a different crowd ... the popular crowd. He dated cheerleaders, got straight A's (even when he didn't earn them!), and became big man on campus. His life went from 0 to 60 overnight, and it was all a blur.

It led to a full scholarship to play ball in college, where he was a solid player. He wasn't quite good enough to play in the NBA, but one of the alumni liked him well enough to make him a VP at his beer company after graduation.

And that was where he met Sandy, a TV model that worked on their commercials, and the woman he would fall in love with and marry.

He finally had everything he wanted, and life was good!

And then one day, while driving his convertible along the beach, his vision blurred, and he blacked out ...

8—ㅜ

When he came to, Stanley was back in Jonas' basement. He had to shake the cobwebs out of his head.

It was only a dream ...

The reality of his actual life smacked him. It was like getting hit on the head with an anvil. For the first time, he felt like ... *somebody*. And now it was gone.

He actually felt like crying.

And then it spoke:

"If only I would have ... "

He couldn't do it again. He couldn't put himself through the pain of living a life that was better than his, only to be taken away.

"If only I would have ... "

What was Jonas thinking? He had invented a torture chamber! Although, it did make sense. Obviously, he had wanted to see what life would have been like if Lilly hadn't died that day.

When he thought about it, Stanley decided that his uncle had invented something incredible. It was a dream machine, and he might be able to make a fortune with it somehow.

"If only I would have ... "

Okay. One more time wouldn't hurt, he thought. *Let's try it again.*

What would be a fun memory to change? Think. Think ...

Yes! The lottery! The day he chose not to play ...

"If only I would have played my lottery numbers instead of watching football!" He was so excited, he screamed the command.

The lights dimmed, the crystals did their thing, and he blacked out ...

⚷—

"Stan! Where the hell you going? The game's about to start!"

Stan didn't want to leave his drunk pal Jimmy, but he had obligations.

"Sorry, J-Man, gotta go. I promised Gloria I'd take her to her mother's, and I gotta stop by the store and pick up a lottery ticket."

"Lottery ticket?! Dude, that's a sucker's bet! No one ever wins."

"Sorry," Stan said, and left the bar.

The next morning, he was awakened by the Gloria's screams. She had just looked up the winning numbers in the paper and saw that they were now millionaires.

They bought a new house, two new cars, and took vacations all over the world. They ate at the best restaurants, and made friends with people that would have never given them the time of day before.

It was a life that neither one of them could have imagined.

They even joined the snooty country club that they both vowed they would never step a foot into. Funny how things change when you have money!

Stan took up golfing and ran with a crowd of corporate execs and entrepreneurs. Gloria began taking tennis lessons and lunching with the wives of powerful men. Their lives revolved around the club, and they were the life of every party.

It was a beautiful day on the back nine that he realized just how great he had it. This was the life he had always wanted.

"Stan, I've got fifty bucks that says you can't sink that putt!"

Robert was one of his new golf buddies at the club. He was also Stan's nemesis on the course. The four-foot putt was usually a no-brainer, but Robert always found a way to add a little pressure.

"Robbie, my friend … you are about to become fifty dollars poorer!"

Stan lined up the putt, made adjustments for the break to the left, and …

His vision blurred.

"Stan? You okay, man?"

"I … I … " And he blacked out.

⚷

His eyes popped open, and once again, he was surrounded by Jonas' dingy basement workshop. This time, though, the disappointment wasn't as cutting. He now knew

91

what his uncle meant when he wrote that this was a greater gift than money ... it would make him both rich and famous!

Stanley stood up and stretched. It seemed like he had been out for days, but in reality it was only twenty minutes or so.

The thought of making millions off this was overwhelming! *Who do I market it to? Who do I tell about it? What do I buy first with the money?* He would never get to sleep tonight.

And then the screen came to life, and the voice once again spoke.

"You have looked at two paths.
Now choose your new life."

This time, the voice had a tone of finality to it.

"Now choose your new life."

"What the hell?" he said to the box. This was ridiculous. He reached over to pull the key out of its home.

It wouldn't budge. In either direction. It was stuck.

"Now choose your new life."

"This isn't funny." Stanley tugged harder at the key, which was a mistake, because it broke off in the slot.

"Now choose your new life."

"Shut up!" He thought about running upstairs, but this was silly. It's just a machine. What could it do?

"It will be chosen for you."

"What? No!"

On the screen, the words "basketball" and "lottery" began to rapidly appear and disappear on the screen. One, then the other, back and forth. Like a carnival wheel. Stanley sat down and stared at the spectacle.

As the exchange began to slow down, the anticipation over which would finally appear was almost too much. The sweat began to pour down his scalp once again.

And then, there was one. Lottery.

It was a good dream-life, but what did this mean?

"Good luck, Stanley."

The lights blew out. Sparks flew from the fixtures, and fizzled into darkness. The hum from the crystal chamber grew, almost at deafening levels, and the lights from the fancy rocks became blinding.

The computers came to life one more time, whirring and spinning. The energy coming from the room was so intense that Stanley felt like he was going to black out.

And then he did.

⚷—

"Stan, that was one hell of a game! That was the first time you broke 80, wasn't it?"

Robert was always Stan's biggest fan, and it was good for his ego.

"Yes it was, Robbie! And, thanks again for the fifty bucks!" He waved the crisp bill above his head, earned for making a simple four-foot putt.

Robert laughed as they headed to the locker room. "Hey, that round went quick. Let's get a drink."

"Love to, my man, but I think I'll surprise Gloria with a little afternoon delight, a la Stan the Man!"

The ride home went quickly. He pulled into the garage, and jumped out of the convertible, excited to see his lovely bride.

She would be so happy that he was home early!

He quietly shut the front door. She wasn't downstairs. *Probably upstairs taking a nap*, he thought. Even better!

Halfway up the steps, he though he heard giggling. Was the TV on? No, it was Gloria.

And someone else. A man.

My God ... a man.

Prepared for the worst, he reached for the bedroom doorknob. His hand was shaking, and his breath caught in his throat.

He threw the door open, and his worst thoughts were realized. Gloria was in bed. With the tennis pro from the club.

What followed after that awkward moment were years of pain and struggle.

In divorce court, Gloria claimed that Stan had ignored her, and she was lonely. She even claimed that he had cheated on her first, which of course wasn't true.

The judge ruled in her favor, and Stan lost nearly everything. The money, the house, the club membership ... but most important, his only love.

What was left, he squandered over the next few years. Savings, investments ... all of it. He even had to sell his car to pay rent. The only thing he could afford was a thirty-year-old Olds that barely ran.

In order to pay the bills, Stan took a job as a security guard at a convenience store making minimum wage. But, he did get to take home the expired beef jerky at the end of each month.

Every night, he would go home to a one-room shack that had hot and cold running brown water. There was a black-and-white TV, and a 40-watt bulb. It wasn't much, but it was his.

And so was a life of regret.

One day, while Stan was working, he thought he saw Gloria driving down the road. It may have, or may not have, been her. These days, he thought he saw her everywhere …

8—⊤

"Stanley? Stanley!"
Earl shook the unconscious man, but to no avail.
"A coma. Just like Jonas."
The old man walked up the stairs, and prepared to make another 911 call, and then the worst call of all … to Gloria.
In the basement, Stanley sat, slumped at the desk. His face was still. A single tear ran down his cheek, and Mr. Paws purred as he rubbed against the motionless leg.

8—⊤

"Phone Home"
By
Christopher J. Valin

My idea came from a story my younger brother told me once about how he had received a phone call from his future self. Tim is a big practical joker and assumed someone was playing a joke on him, but apparently the other Tim told him some things nobody else could have known and he ended up believing it to be true. I thought it would make a great basis for a time travel story, so I wrote out the basic plot about how the character got the phone call and eventually came to make the call. I wasn't sure where to go from there until some of the others in this group threw out some great ideas, including the main character running into himself. I started thinking about how most time travel stories are neatly wrapped up at the end and decided to go in the opposite direction ...

As approaching footsteps echoed down the hall, Todd quickly hid around the corner. He slowly peeked out to see who it was, and saw *himself* approaching, wearing the exact same clothes he had on and looking back to see who was following *him*. Todd stuck out his leg and tripped his other self, who fell flat on his face. The other Todd looked up and backed away in shock as he saw who had tripped him up. "You – y-you're – "

"*You*. Right. Now listen, you can't – " Second Todd wasn't interested. He popped First Todd in the face, knocking him back to where he had been hiding, and ran for a nearby security door. Second Todd looked at the lock mechanism on the door, then pulled out a key card and swiped it.

First Todd started to get up, but heard more footsteps coming down the hall and hid again as Second Todd ran through the open doorway.

Todd leaned against the wall, looked up in frustration, and shook his head to himself. *Not again.*

8—т

Todd peeked around the ice machine and looked into the dining area. Jeff's break was just about over, so he'd be standing up any second. Todd tried to stifle a laugh as he watched the tall, thin waiter try to get up from his seat at the booth.

As expected, Jeff wasn't able to stand.

"What the … ?" Jeff realized he was stuck to the seat. "Son of a – " He also knew immediately who had glued him to it. "Todd!"

Todd couldn't hold it in any more. He leaned against the ice machine and busted out in loud guffaws as Jeff started screaming from the other part of the restaurant.

Then he realized something was wrong. Jeff wasn't just angry, he was in pain.

"Aaaaahhhh! It's burning! Someone call 911!"

8—т

"How was I supposed to know the super glue would soak through his pants?"

In the parking lot, a couple of medics were pushing Jeff on a gurney. Jeff was face down with his rear in the air as they loaded him onto the ambulance.

Todd wasn't getting any sympathy from his manager. "You shouldn't *have* to know, because you shouldn't use it for something like that."

"You have to admit, though, I really got him good this time."

"Todd, Jeff's going to be out of work for at least a few days. Sometimes funny just isn't worth it."

"Dude, he plays practical jokes on me all the time!" Todd thought back to the last one, when Jeff had closed the lid to the ice machine just as Todd was about to dump a tub of ice into it. The ice had spilled out all over the floor and Todd was cleaning and mopping for what felt like a couple of hours.

"You were never injured like this, Todd."

"So ... what? I'm getting written up again?"

"I've already gone that route a couple more times than I'm supposed to. I'm afraid I'm going to have to let you go."

Todd looked incredulous. "Let me go? Like *fire* me?"

"You'll be lucky if Jeff doesn't press charges, too. I need you to get your stuff, clock out, and go home." The manager went back into the restaurant.

Todd turned and watched as they closed the doors to the ambulance and despite himself, he started laughing again and shook his head as he went inside.

8—⟊

The ringing started out as part of Todd's dream until it finally woke him up. He looked at his clock: 3:44 a.m. *Who the hell is calling this late? Or is it this early?*

He started searching for the cordless phone, digging through piles of clothes. He finally found it and hit the button to answer.   "Yeah, hello, who – ?"

"Shut up and listen, I don't have much time. I know you're gonna think this is a practical joke, but it isn't. You have to do what I say. *Don't use the key.* Got that? When the time comes, don't use it!"

"Who is this? Is this Jeff? What – "

"Just don't forget, Todd! You have to re – " Click. The call ended.

Todd looked at the phone for a moment. Too tired to figure it out, he tossed the phone back into the pile of clothes and was asleep as soon as his head hit the pillow.

Weeks went by, and Todd still couldn't find a job. His unemployment wasn't enough to pay his bills, and there was nothing in the want ads for him. With all the chain restaurants closing down in Vegas, cooks were a dime a dozen.

Then he saw it: *Participants wanted for scientific study. Easy money. No experience necessary. Call now!*

"I certainly qualify for that job." He tore out the ad and started looking for his phone again.

As he followed the directions to the facility through the desert, Todd realized he was in the middle of nowhere and started wondering if he'd have enough gas to get back home. He took a number of twists and turns down some old roads and finally saw something ahead. It was a series of aged, brick government buildings and airplane hangars surrounded by electrified chain-link fences and patrolled by heavily armed guards with unmarked black uniforms and very big dogs. After reading the sign out front that said *No unauthorized personnel admitted* he began to wonder if maybe he was in the wrong place.

Todd pulled up to the guardhouse next to the gate and the guard looked at him suspiciously. "Name."

"Todd Vandergroot."

The guard squinted at a list on a computer screen, looked at Todd again, then back at the screen.

The gate began to open and, without a word, the guard waved him through.

The balding, bespectacled scientist was nice enough, but seemed very absorbed in his project. Still, Todd was a little nervous. "So is this gonna be some kind of psychological experiment or something?"

"Something like that," replied the scientist absentmindedly. He was hooking Todd up to some equipment that began measuring his vital signs on several monitors around the room.

"They didn't really tell me much at the interview."

"That's because the people who interviewed you don't know much. We just give them a list of questions and they give us your answers."

"So I guess I must've done pretty well."

"Huh?"

Todd thought it was obvious. "In the interview."

The scientist looked at him for a moment. "Uh ... yeah. Yeah, you're perfect." The man continued looking at the readings and writing things down.

Todd noticed a key card sitting on the desk next to some of the scientist's other belongings and couldn't resist playing a joke on the guy. He slowly reached over and put the plastic card in his pocket. "This place is pretty cool. How come I couldn't find it on Google Maps?"

"Top secret."

Todd smiled. "Sure. Like 'Area 51' or something, right?"

The scientist raised an eyebrow and looked at him suspiciously, stopping his work for the first time. But he still didn't answer.

"How long does this take? 'Cause, like, I'm supposed to go out with some friends later, and – "

"You might want to forget about that. You're going to be here a while." Something about the way the scientist said "a while" made him even more nervous.

"Okay, well, they said no cell phones or anything allowed, so is there a landline I can use to call and let them know, or … ?"

"Ah … sorry, no one's allowed to call out from here."

The scientist went back to work, then suddenly stopped what he was doing. "These friends of yours … they're not the type to ask a lot of questions are they?"

"Ha. My friends? They – " Todd realized what he was saying. "They, well, hmmm, now that you mention it, a couple of them might, I don't know, do some investigating if anything … happened … to me or … something."

The scientist raised another eyebrow as he stared into Todd's eyes. "Wait right here. I'll be right back." He opened the door. "Don't go anywhere."

As soon as the scientist was out the door, Todd jumped out of his seat and began pulling the wires off of himself. *Okay, okay, one step at a time here … find a phone, call for help, then hide out until the cavalry arrives …*

He opened the door slowly and looked carefully out into the hallway. There was nobody around, but he still tried to be nonchalant as he walked down the hall in case there were cameras on him.

Just as he was almost in the clear, he heard the scientist's voice: "Hey! Get back here!"

Todd took off running and turned a corner, but realized that if he were on camera, he'd never be able to lose anyone. At the end of the hall, he arrived at a heavy, locked door with a red light flashing and a sign that said *Restricted Area: Level 5 Clearance and Above Only*.

The scientist was panicking. "We're not going to hurt you! I promise! *Don't go in there!*"

Pulling the key card out of his pocket, Todd noticed it had a bright red 5 on it, so he tried sliding it through the lock mechanism just as some guards came up behind the scientist. The door slid open and he made it through just as it closed on his pursuers.

Inside the enormous restricted warehouse area, he saw rows of strange machines and what looked like exotic sea creatures and giant insects inside of huge glass tubes full of some kind of liquid.

"Holy … " As he stood frozen in silence, he heard the guards coming in through the door. Todd started running and turned down one of the rows. They were right behind him, and he started to panic as he got to the end.

Standing next to one of the large tubes, Todd grabbed a metal instrument that looked like an alien vacuum cleaner and swung it as hard as he could into the glass container. Strange liquid came rushing out and blocked the guards from reaching him. Further down the row, he saw the scientist's face go pale. The man started to run, but tripped and fell to the ground.

Todd turned to see what the scientist was running away from and immediately felt the blood rush from his face and his stomach clench into a ball. Standing next to him was a creature that made the Queen in *Aliens* look like a children's cartoon. Nine feet tall, slimy, and covered in spikes, it had multiple eyes like a spider and the fangs of a saber-toothed tiger. Just as it was about to turn on him, the guards began shooting at it, and it went after them.

Todd took the opportunity to run, and tried to help the scientist up on his way down the row. Behind him, he heard the horrifying screams of the guards. He didn't bother to turn to see what was causing the tearing and shredding sounds that followed.

There were no more screams from the guards.

Todd and the scientist ran as they heard wet footsteps increasing in speed behind them. They reached the door, but it was shut tight again.

The scientist could barely speak as he tried to catch his breath. "Do you still have the key?"

Todd felt around in his pockets, but couldn't find it. He must have dropped it somewhere during the chase. He shook his head.

"Then there's only one other option." The man pointed toward the farthest row of machinery and they ran. The creature's growls and footsteps continued behind them.

They reached what appeared to be a large potbelly stove with a windowed door in it and a small console connected to it by large wires and tubes. It looked like a steampunk version of a Tardis.

As the sounds of the creature continued to grow nearer, the scientist handed Todd a cell phone. "Listen carefully. I'm going to send you back in time, but not far."

"Wh-what? To when?"

"I don't have time to make exact calculations. Whenever you end up, just call and warn someone – anyone. Got it?"

They could see the creature as it began coming down their row quickly. "Get in there!" The scientist began pushing buttons and turning knobs as Todd opened the door and jumped in. Through the small window, he saw the creature about to come upon the scientist and he wondered if the man would be able to finish setting it in time. He heard a locking mechanism activate inside the door.

Despite what was coming, he saw the scientist smile as he hit one last button. In the next second, the creature took the man's head off with one swipe of his claw, like a golf ball leaving the tee. The creature looked Todd in the eye and started toward the machine as it hummed and started to shake. Todd wondered if the door would hold as he backed away from it, then tripped over something.

To his shock and horror, he saw his own dead body lying next to him, in the early stages of decomposition. "What the fu – "

Slam! The creature began pounding on the door. Todd couldn't decide if he was more scared of the creature or sitting next to his own corpse. His heart began pounding so hard he thought it was going to burst from his chest.

The door looked as if it was about to give way, when suddenly there was a bright light and the feeling of rocketing down the track on a roller coaster.

Todd passed out.

Todd woke up and wondered how long he had been out. He stood up, feeling groggy, and looked out the door. There was no sign of the scientist or the creature. He tried to open the door, but the handle wouldn't budge. He put all his might behind it, but still no luck.

He was trapped.

Staying as far away from his doppelganger as he could, he opened the cell phone and dialed the first number he could think of and waited. "C'mon ... pick up! Pick up!" He looked at the battery icon and saw it empty and flashing.

He heard his own voice answer. "Yeah, hello, who – ?"

"Shut up and listen, I don't have much time. I know you're gonna think this is a practical joke, but it isn't. You have to do what I say. *Don't use the key.* Got that? When the time comes, don't use it!"

"Who is this? Is this Jeff? What – "

"Just don't forget, Todd! You have to re – " Click. He looked at the phone. It had died.

He threw the phone against the inside of the machine, and it smashed to pieces. Todd stared at the corpse and wondered how long he had before he ran out of air. He tried pulling on the door again, but it was stuck tight. He looked through the small window, desperately searching for any sign of a person outside.

He almost had a heart attack as his own face suddenly appeared on the other side of the window. This Third Todd started turning the handle on the outside of the door. He pounded on the window and pointed down for First Todd to do the same. Todd got up and they tried turning it together.

Finally it began to move.

Once the door was open, Third Todd grabbed him. "I can't explain everything right now, you'll just have to trust

107

me. I've been doing this a while, and I think I have it figured out."

He reached into his pocket and pulled out a cell phone battery. "Where's the phone?"

First Todd glanced back at the bits of plastic and circuitry on the floor of the time machine. He slowly pointed at it.

"Damn. Why do we always do that?" Third Todd began pacing back and forth. "Okay, how about the key card?"

"No, but it has to be in here somewhere."

"Actually it won't be, because you haven't lost it yet. But don't worry, I have a few extras."

8—⊤

The identical men were discussing how they were going to proceed when they heard a strange humming noise that Third Todd recognized as the time machine in action.

When Fourth Todd appeared, they explained the situation to him. He was confused about one thing, though. "How come all of us aren't appearing at the exact same time?"

First Todd didn't have a clue, but Third Todd had it figured it out. "Every time it happens, events are slightly different. The scientist dude didn't have time to be exact, so the tiniest difference causes us to go back to different points in the past."

"When the hell did we get so smart?"

"I didn't do it on my own. There were other Todds around even longer trying to figure this whole thing out."

The other two Todds answered simultaneously. "*Were?*"

Third Todd shook his head. "You don't wanna know."

Fourth Todd spoke up. "Maybe we do."

Third Todd sighed and led his twins down a long row of machinery and artifacts until he got to a giant freezer in back. He swiped the key card and opened the door.

When the frozen cloud dispersed, they could see dozens of dead Todds, some in relatively decent shape, others missing body parts or completely torn to shreds.

First Todd was nervous now. "Exactly how many times have we tried this kind of thing?"

"I don't know. But it's a lot, and most of us don't make it through. Every time we seem to have it down, something goes wrong. We've tried calling ourselves at various points, stopping ourselves from coming in here in different ways, escaping from this facility ... and half the time it's another one of us who messes everything up. But I think I've finally figured out a way that will work."

Third Todd shut the door. "Here's the plan ... "

First Todd stayed hidden around the corner as the scientist and the guards arrived at the security door where Second Todd had just gone through, and the guards finally got the door open. Since he had failed to stop the new him from entering the room, the plan was shot – he'd have to improvise.

Just as the guards got the door open and went through, Todd jumped out of hiding and grabbed the scientist by the back of his lab coat. He threw him down and sat on the small man's chest.

The scientist's eyes went wide. "Wha – I thought – "

Todd covered his mouth. "Stop talking. If you don't do what I say, you're dead."

It seemed like an eternity before the monster was loose and the shots and screaming began. Todd took his hand off the scientist's mouth. "Hear that? I just saved your life. Now follow me ... "

Todd barely had enough time to explain things to the scientist before they got to the time machine. Since the scientist wasn't there to direct the latest Todd to the machine, the creature would be chasing him around elsewhere in the warehouse.

"Remember, take your time and make sure you send me back far enough. If this works, none of this will have ever happened." Todd opened the door to the time machine and recoiled as he smelled the rotting corpse. To the scientist's dismay, he pulled the corpse from the chamber and left it sitting right in front of the machine. Todd pointed to his dead clone. "And make sure you set it for the door to unlock so I'm not trapped in there again."

Through the small window, Todd could see himself being torn limb from limb by the creature at the other end of the warehouse. Would there be enough time for the scientist to get the calculations right this time?

The bright light and lurching feeling didn't hit him by surprise this time, but they were just as dramatic and he still passed out.

When Todd awoke, he immediately checked the door and saw that he was able to get out. He checked the guard schedule Third Todd had given to him and matched it against the time on the retro-tech console for the time machine. Just right.

He stood next to the door and waited for the guard to arrive on his routine check, heavy object at the ready. When the guy came through, he didn't even have time to register the presence of another person before Todd knocked him out cold. Todd changed into his uniform, which worked despite being a little too big except for around the waist, where it was really snug. Luckily, these guys even wore shades indoors.

Between the uniform and the key card, getting out wasn't much of a problem. In fact, Todd was practically home free before he ran into his only problem during his escape – another him. Apparently, this Todd had come up with the same idea of stealing a guard's uniform and didn't realize who he was attacking when he leaped from hiding and knocked First Todd to the ground.

Fifth Todd lifted his fist and was about to hit him again. "Wait, Todd! It's me!"

The newer Todd pulled off the dark glasses and saw his own face. "Jesus, man, what the hell is going on here?"

First Todd tried to summarize the whole thing as fast as possible. Fifth Todd agreed to go along with the plan, and even provide a diversion inside while First Todd was getting out of the compound.

"Just one thing," he said. "What happens to us if your plan works?"

First Todd shrugged. "Dunno. I guess we all disappear. What do you think?"

"Sounds right to me, I guess."

⊙━┱

"Depends on what you want to use it for," said the old man behind the counter.

"Well, I'm gonna be gluing cloth to plastic." Todd was holding up two different types of super glue.

"I'd say they're 'bout the same. Go with the cheaper one."

"Sounds good." Todd paid for the glue and left the store giddy with anticipation for his next practical joke. He read the instructions on the package of the super glue on his way down the alley to the parking lot in back, and realized someone was blocking his way.

"'Scuse me."

"Look at me," said a familiar voice.

Todd almost fell back when he saw himself standing in front of him. "Man, you almost gave me a heart attack." He stood up close to the other Todd and looked his face over.

"Dude, that is awesome. Who put you up to this? Is that, like, a professional makeup job, or prosthetics, or what?"

111

"No. Listen to me … "

"Man, there's no way they found someone that looks *that* much like me. No frikkin' way."

"Todd, I *am* you. I'm from the future."

Todd busted out laughing. "This is freakin' great! Is there a camera? Am I being punk'd or something?" He was looking around the alley for some sign of recording devices.

The look-alike took hold of him by the front of his shirt. "You have to follow my instructions. *Don't* pull that prank on Jeff, *don't* go looking at ads in the newspaper, and most of all *don't* go volunteering for any experiments for some extra cash."

Todd pulled his twin's hands off his shirt. "Look, I don't know who you think you are, but this is getting out of hand. I'm gonna do what I want, and some actor hired by Jeff isn't gonna scare me off, no matter how much you look like me."

Angry, Todd began stalking down the alley toward his car. Desperate, First Todd picked up a cement block and broke it over his head. He fell like a sack of potatoes and blood began streaming from his ears. First Todd checked for a pulse. The other him was dead.

First Todd expected to disappear from reality now that there was no way for this version of himself to exist. He looked at his hands, expecting them to start fading away, but nothing happened.

After making sure nobody was around, First Todd put the other Todd's body into a dumpster full of compost. He made sure it was completely covered and wondered what would happen if the body was found. *Well, if they identify the body as me, I'll just have to show them that they're wrong.*

As he was about to walk away, Todd noticed a bag on the ground and picked it up. He pulled out the super glue and looked it over, and couldn't help smiling at the practical joke he remembered playing … even though it would never actually happen now.

He tossed the glue into the dumpster and walked to his car. After all, he didn't want to be late for work.

112

"Pretty Was Her Face"
By
Eugene Ramos

When we decided to write our next book around
Carolee's idea of keys, several scenarios came to mind. A few
involved automatons requiring keys to function – a toy
soldier, a steampunk robot, a dancer in a music box.
From all the ideas that soon overcrowded my head, I
wanted, most of all, to write something that was completely
different from my entry in The Artifact, *which was a hard sci-*
fi short story requiring a lot of research in archaeology, code
breaking, and Martian meteorology. I wanted this time to tell
a simple story about love. So, with equal parts Shakespeare
and Grimm (and a dash of Sting), I fashioned a little fairy tale
about a beautiful princess locked in her father's dungeon and
the man who possessed the key to her heart.

Many, many years ago, in a land whose name has long
since been forgotten, there lived a King who lost his Queen to
the brutality of soulless men. Wanting to protect his young
daughter from such cruelty, he confined her to his castle's
dungeon. When she asked why, she was simply told that, like
her mother, pretty was her face. For thirteen years the Princess
lived in the darkness of her prison, unseen by anybody except
for her father and her jailer. However, on the Princess's
eighteenth birthday, the King decreed to the kingdoms beyond
his own that he would entertain suitors for his daughter's hand
in marriage. The King's subjects rejoiced, for their ruler was
old of age and had no heir apparent.

From far and wide, princes journeyed to the kingdom,
brought on by rumors of the Princess's unparalleled beauty.
But rumors they were not, for, as the princes learned upon

their arrival, the Princess had blossomed into an exceedingly beautiful woman with hair as red as flame and skin as white as pearl. Her eyes were like polished cobalt, captivating all who would but look her way. Every prince who had laid eyes upon her pledged his undying love for her.

But love alone would not win the Princess's hand. The King devised a lottery by which each prince had to choose a key from a lot of five score keys. But only one key, the King pronounced, would unlock the door to the Princess's prison.

"Why leave such a union to Chance?" the princes wondered.

"Only one man is destined to marry my daughter," the King stated, "and Fate shall guide his hand to the correct key."

As the keys were laid out before them upon a slate of black marble in the King's throne room, each prince eyed the next with a degree of distrust and distaste, believing himself to be the Destined One. Each of the keys was different. There were keys of gold, keys of silver, and keys of lead, each encrusted with precious stones of diamond, ruby, and emerald. The princes studied them by the light of the hearth's fire, searching for any clue that might lead them to the correct key. One bold prince, the Prince of Caudwell, grabbed a golden key and demanded that he go first. With the King's consent, Caudwell ventured forth into the depths of the dungeon alone. Breath bated, the other princes waited for the outcome of Caudwell's choice. Long moments passed, and Caudwell emerged, his eyes downcast, his swagger lost, his heart broken. The Princess was not delivered.

Having witnessed Caudwell's failure, one prince refused to let Chance decide his fate. Prince Richard of Deering, who came from a kingdom not far hence, had a friend who was a locksmith. They had been acquainted since they were children – the young Prince and his Pauper friend – but to each other, they were like brothers. The two of them used to lay out in the fields at night and stare at the stars, dreaming about their futures.

118

"I want to become a king," the Pauper had told the Prince.

The Prince couldn't help but laugh. "You can't become a king. Only I can become a king."

"Why?" the Pauper asked.

"Because I'm a prince," he told him, "and you are not."

The Pauper didn't understand what that had to do with his wanting to become a king. What made him so different from the Prince? The answer to that question, however, soon became quite evident. The Prince, unlike the Pauper, lived in a citadel, wore fine clothing, and ate lavish meals. The Pauper, unlike the Prince, lived in a small cottage, wore clothes of gruff fabrics, and ate modest meals. He didn't know why such disparity existed. Only that it did. This unfairness made him covet things he didn't have. And soon the Pauper became a thief.

At first he stole things that he felt, in a fair world, he deserved – toys and trinkets and shiny little things. And then he moved on to more expensive items, picking pockets, purloining purses, and nicking necklaces. As he got older, he discovered that people kept their most treasured possessions behind lock and key. So he apprenticed himself to a locksmith who taught him the art of tumblers and bolts and pins and levers. And by studying the inner workings of locks, the Pauper learned how to break them.

Although he had perfected the art of lock picking, the Pauper had yet to perfect the art of caution. One night, while robbing the residence of a prominent Lord, the Pauper was caught off guard by the sight of the Lord's wife in the act of removing her corset. The Lord's men apprehended him, and the Lord demanded justice for his indignity. Death was the punishment for the crime of theft. However, the Prince intervened on his friend's behalf and pardoned him. The Pauper was given a second chance, and he grew up to become a law-abiding locksmith. And now the Prince had come to ask the Locksmith to return the favor.

119

The Prince invited the Locksmith to dine at his citadel, whereupon he extolled the physical attributes of the Princess.

"How pretty is her face?" the Locksmith wondered.

"The most beautiful you have ever seen," marveled the Prince. "I want her as my wife."

"What would you have me do?" asked the Locksmith.

"The Princess is locked within the King's dungeon," the Prince replied. "Make me a key that would set her free."

The Locksmith went to work on the Prince's request, but created something more than was expected of him. While the key would indeed be able to release the Princess from her confinement, the Locksmith had other designs in mind. Unbeknownst to anyone, the Locksmith had kept a secret room in his workshop where he hid a collection of items he had stolen in his youth – priceless stones, gold jewelry, the finest royal livery. He yearned to add more to his collection. So he forged a key unlike any he had forged before. A key that would unlock any door. A master key. And with this master key, he would have access to any door he wanted to enter and egress from any confining situation he wanted to escape. And he wanted desperately to escape the unrewarding life he lived.

With the key cast, the Locksmith decided to test it, not only on the locks that confined the Princess but also on the vaults that secured the King's treasures. Concealed within a red cloak, he journeyed to the King's castle under the cover of night. When he arrived at the castle, he eluded the guards without effort, for there were few who were awake. Although the corridors were labyrinthine, there was no door that could stand between his key and the dungeon below. Finding the Princess's prison cell was the easiest of the tasks, for there were no other prisoners in the dungeon and no guard keeping watch. He approached the prison door and slipped his key into the lock. With a turn the door sighed open. The Locksmith smiled, for the master key had worked.

As he closed the door to lock it shut, he dropped the key and awakened the Princess as it clattered to the stone floor.

She stepped out of bed and approached him, the bars of her prison door the only thing separating them.

"Who are you?" she asked.

"Nobody," the Locksmith answered.

"Take me with you," she pleaded.

"I cannot."

"But you have opened my prison with your key," she said. "I am yours."

The Locksmith made the mistake of looking into her cobalt eyes. And before he could utter another word, he was smitten. Nay, he was in love.

The Princess reached across the bars to caress the Locksmith's hand, but he quickly pulled his hand back.

"I cannot, my Princess," he told her with a heavy heart. "This key does not belong to me."

"Then to whom?" she asked.

The Locksmith stood there a moment, torn in two. The Princess was the most beautiful thing he had ever seen, and he wanted her more than anything he had ever desired. But he made a promise, a promise he intended to keep.

"Please stay," the Princess implored, her hands folded in front of her chest in prayer. "I have not spoken to anyone besides my father and my jail keeper for many years."

"I must leave," he said as he turned his back on her. But the sound of thunder froze him in place, and hard rain began to pelt against the stone façade of the castle.

"It's raining," the Princess said. "Stay … at least until the rain ceases."

So he did.

The Locksmith and the Princess spoke for many hours, long after the rain had stopped. She was eager to hear of his life, far away from the walls of her dungeon. She giggled like a little girl at the stories he told her of his misadventures as a young thief. And the Locksmith found that he could not stop talking. He wanted nothing more than to see her smile and hear her laugh. It was soon morning when the Princess reached out beyond her cage to touch the Locksmith's hand again. This time he did not move.

"Take me with you," she said.

As the Locksmith was about to speak, footfalls were heard coming down the steps and into the dungeon. The Princess's face turned white. "The Witch! You must hide!" she said. "Don't let her find you." So the Locksmith found an empty cell, locked the door, and withdrew into the darkest of corners.

From where he stood, the Locksmith watched a dark-skinned Emir enter the dungeon, flanked by two castle guards. He was dressed in long, flowing white garments, and in his right hand he bore a silver key. "My Princess," he said in an accent the Locksmith did not recognize. "I have come to make you my bride." He placed his key into the lock, but the key would not turn.

"I am sorry," the Princess stated.

"Not as sorry as I," the Emir said with a huff.

As he turned to leave, he came face-to-face with a haggard Old Woman, whom the Locksmith did not see enter. She was wrapped in a dark blue pelisse. But it was her eyes that grabbed the Locksmith's attention. They were blacker than the blackest pit he had ever seen.

"Make way, Old Woman," the Emir said.

"What poor manners for a Prince from the High Sahara!" the Old Woman exclaimed. Her opened mouth was like a darkened cave full of stalactites and stalagmites. "I shall have to teach you some."

The castle guards grabbed the Emir's arms. "What is the meaning of this?" he demanded. But no one answered him. Instead, the Old Woman touched his face, almost lovingly. Suddenly, the Emir screamed in pain. It was the loudest scream that the Locksmith had ever heard. He watched in horror as blood trickled down the Old Woman's hands and wrists. And suddenly he saw the unimaginable – the Old Woman was holding the Emir's face in her hands as if it were

122

a mask. The Emir's piercing scream ceased as he collapsed to the ground, dead.

"Who would like to be the Prince of the High Sahara?" the Old Woman inquired.

The guard closest to the Locksmith simply nodded. She caressed the guard's cheek and his face shed off his head like so much discarded skin. With great care, she placed the Emir's face on the guard and bid him to serve his King well. He then left the dungeon to tell the other princes that he, the Prince of the High Sahara, had failed to release the Princess.

After the Old Woman and the remaining guard left the dungeon with the Emir's corpse, the Locksmith cautiously exited his cage and found the Princess weeping silently. "What has happened?" he asked, his voice full of fear.

The Princess regained her composure and said, "You must leave now before the Witch returns. But come back tonight when all is asleep, and I will have a tale to tell you."

The Locksmith returned to the castle after nightfall and found the Princess waiting for him patiently within her prison cell. She smiled widely upon his approach and bid him to join her inside. He was reluctant, but he soon relented. He unlocked the door, and she led him to her bed, where they sat.

"When I was five years of age, my mother was murdered," the Princess began her tale. Soon after her mother's burial, her father, the King, had gone out on his own to find those responsible for the Queen's death. Upon his journey, he found himself lost in a vast forest. He followed the rays of the sun hoping to find a path out. The light led him to a clearing where he found a beautiful woman bathing in a river. The woman looked uncannily like the Queen, so the King approached her. Before the river's edge, the woman's clothing laid scattered about. Among her belongings was a golden armlet that caught his eye and enchanted him. It contained in its center a large red jewel that sparkled in the sunlight. When he placed it on his wrist and wore it as a bracer, the beautiful woman shrieked and transformed into an ugly Witch. She cursed the King, but he knew that her threats were empty for he had in his possession the source of her power. The Witch had become his servant.

With the Witch now under his control, the King urged her to tell him who the Queen's murderers were, but she did not know. Her powers were limited without her armlet. All she could tell him was that the killers were of royal blood. Incensed, the King wanted to declare war on the neighboring kingdoms, but the Witch counseled him to be patient. She advised him not to pursue the culprits but to let them come to him. So the King devised a plan, a trap that would satisfy his thirst for revenge and feed his newfound hunger for control and power. However, this trap could not be sprung until the time was right.

"I am the trap," the Princess told the Locksmith.

The Locksmith did not understand why the King would kill all the princes and replace them with lackeys whom he could control. To the Princess, on the other hand, the reason was perfectly clear. Her father wanted simply to protect his daughter. But she knew that he was misguided. She knew that what he was doing was wrong. She knew that somehow the jewel on his bracer was twisting his good intentions.

"Your father must be stopped," said the Locksmith.

"I know, and I have a plan," the Princess said. "You must marry me."

"I cannot."

"You must," the Princess maintained. "It is the only way we can obtain the bracer."

"There must be another way," the Locksmith argued.

"If we wed, by custom, my father must grant me one wish," the Princess told the Locksmith. "I will ask for his bracer, and then we can destroy it."

"I'm sorry, Princess," the Locksmith said as he backed out of the prison cell and locked the door behind him. "There must be another way."

The Locksmith found himself in a situation from which there was no apparent escape. He returned home to ponder the dilemma, to study its tumblers and bolts, its pins and levers. Every lock, he knew, had a key to unlock it. The solution, however, proved elusive. And the appearance of his friend, the Prince, only made matters worse.

"Where is the key?" the Prince asked.

"The key is not yet ready," replied the Locksmith.

"Then why have I spied you at the castle on more than one occasion?" the Prince challenged.

"I was there merely to test the key."

"You were there to steal the Princess!"

The Locksmith denied the accusations, but the Prince didn't believe him, for there was many a time when the Locksmith had stolen from the Prince. When the Prince demanded the key, the Locksmith refused him.

"If I give you the key, you will die," the Locksmith told the Prince.

"Do not threaten me," the Prince warned.

The friends fought – the Prince for the Princess's heart and the Locksmith for the Prince's life. They traded blow for blow, but the Prince was the better of the two. And when it was over, the Prince stood triumphant.

"I thought we were brothers," the Prince cast his angered gaze down upon the beaten Locksmith. "You have broken my heart."

The Prince took the key from the Locksmith and departed for the castle. When the Prince returned to Deering without the Princess, the Locksmith knew that his friend was dead. With his promise to the Prince no longer impeding him, the tumblers and levers began to fall into place.

Like every locksmith worth his weight in precious stone, the Locksmith made a copy of every key he cast. This too was true of his master key. And he would need it in order for the

Princess's plan to work. But before returning to the castle, it was also necessary for him to play the part of a prince, so he went to his secret room hidden within his workshop to transform himself. From his collection of loot, the Locksmith dressed himself in raiment of royal blue and scarlet red. From his chest of jewelry, he found a ring with the royal seal of Deering. And from his armory of stolen arsenal, he chose a sword that had the ideal heft and weight to exact his revenge against the Witch. When he arrived at the castle, he was announced as Prince Spencer, brother of Prince Richard of Deering.

In front of the King's court and the invited princes, the Locksmith was asked to select a key from the lot laid out before him. He chose the one that looked the most like his master key – a silver one with a stone of amethyst. An escort of two royal guards led him to the dungeon. As they neared the Princess's cell, the Locksmith placed one hand on the hilt of his sword, ready to face the Witch when she appeared. When the Princess saw the Locksmith dressed in royal finery, she stood up from her bed, a look of surprise across her face. The Locksmith placed a single finger against his lips.

"I have come to set you free, Princess," he said.

With a subtle flick on his wrist, the Locksmith slipped the silver key into his sleeve and retrieved the master key. He placed the key into the lock, turned it, and pushed the prison door open. The Princess then ran into the arms of her prince.

"I knew you would come back," she whispered into his ear.

"Was there ever any doubt?" he said before he kissed her across the lips.

The two were so overjoyed that neither questioned the whereabouts of the Witch.

When the Locksmith re-entered the throne room with the Princess at his side, there was an audible gasp from the other princes. Their opportunity to wed the fairest woman in the Lands was now gone, and they each cursed their procrastination. While the atmosphere within the castle was decidedly negative, outside it was a different story. Bells tolled throughout the kingdom, and town criers took to the streets announcing the news that a prince had set the Princess free. A celebration was at hand.

The wedding was a pompous affair, resplendent with flowers of all type and decoration of all manner. As befitting a man of royal birth, the Locksmith was given new garments to wear: a white cape of the finest fabric, a gold-plated suit of armor, and a crown encrusted with the rarest of jewels. The nuptials were attended by all members of the King's court, including the jilted princes and members of their retinue. Outside of the castle, the King's subjects awaited eagerly for the royal couple to make their first public appearance. When the Locksmith and the Princess stepped out onto the balcony overlooking the crowd as husband and wife, there was such a loud cheer that the ground shook for many, many miles around. The Locksmith took a moment from all the joyous commotion that surrounded him and smiled at his beautiful Princess.

When all the ceremonies were done and all the guests had departed, the King called forth his daughter and his new son-in-law to the throne room, where the fire in the hearth kept the cold of night at bay. The King asked the Locksmith to kneel before him so that he could be knighted into the King's army. However, instead of feeling the flat of the King's sword gracing each of his shoulders, he felt the point of the blade pushing against his throat.

"Tell me," the King demanded, "how you opened a lock which no key was meant to open."

The Locksmith said, "I fashioned my own key that can open any door."

"So you admit that you cheated," the King said as he pressed his sword harder against the Locksmith's neck. "Convince me why you deserve to live when you have ruined my plans and stolen my daughter."

"I have not," the Locksmith said as he raised his eyes to meet the King's. "I have set you and the Princess free."

"Free?" the King laughed. "Free from what?"

"The Witch's thrall."

"The Witch has no control over me," the King declared. "My actions are my own."

"Then prove it," the Princess spoke. "Give me your bracer."

"I cannot," the King replied.

"But you must," said the Princess. "It is my nuptial wish."

Despite his misgivings, the King could not refuse his daughter. He sheathed his sword and turned his prized possession over to the Princess. When she curled her fingers around the bracer, the Locksmith witnessed something disturbing. Her cobalt eyes for a moment flickered to obsidian black. As she placed the bracer around her upper arm, the Locksmith's heart broke. He withdrew his sword and cut the Princess's arm off.

The King screamed in horror, "What have you done to my daughter?"

The young woman cackled, revealing the broken and jagged teeth that littered her mouth. With her one arm raised, she hauled the Locksmith with an invisible force and threw him across the chamber. She then picked up her severed limb and re-attached it to her shoulder. It was as if the arm had not been severed in the first place.

The King called out for his guards, but the Witch shut his mouth and barred the doors shut.

"Now, my liege, I will have my revenge." From afar the Witch lifted the King off his throne and proceeded to squeeze the life out of him. "Your kingdom will now be mine."

But before she could finish her deed, she found one half of a sword protruding from her chest. She spun around and found the Locksmith behind her. She grabbed him by his neck and picked him up.

"What have you done with the Princess?" the Locksmith demanded as he clutched desperately at his perpetrator's arm.

"The same thing I did to the Queen," the Witch said through her craggy grin. "I took her face."

The Locksmith screamed in anguish as he struggled in the Witch's grasp. He kicked hard against the sword in her chest, causing her to flinch in pain and drop him.

"Fool, you cannot defeat me," the Witch said.

From the floor, the Locksmith raised his hand and showed her the red jewel he had filched from her armlet.

"No!" she screamed.

The Witch reached for his hand, but it was too late. The Locksmith had thrown the jewel into the fire. As the Witch hurried to the hearth, the jewel cracked inside the fire's intense heat, and suddenly the Witch seemed smaller. She was powerful no more.

The Locksmith, battered and bloody but not beaten, stalked toward the Witch and pulled his sword from her back. And as the Witch fell to her knees, the Locksmith raised his sword above his head. The face of the Princess looked pleadingly up at him, and the Locksmith hesitated.

"I was too late, my love," he said. "And for that, I am sorry."

He brought the sword swiftly down across the Witch's neck, severing her head from her shoulders. With one hard kick, he sent the Witch's body into the fire. When the decapitated head rolled to a stop, the Princess's face looked up at the Locksmith without warmth and without pity.

The Witch was dead, and her hold over the King and his kingdom was at an end. Even so, the King passed away two days later. Weighed down by the truth of his wife's death and the loss of his daughter, the King's heart simply stopped beating. The day after his death, the Locksmith became the newly crowned King. He had gotten his boyhood wish.

Over the next three years, the new King exposed the pretenders that the former King and the Witch had planted and brought peace throughout the Lands. In his kingdom, his rule was fair and just. Nobody lacked. Nobody wanted. The privilege of the few became the privilege of many. As a result, he was beloved by his subjects and was an enemy of no one.

As his days grew short, he took a commoner as his wife and made her his queen. He was a kind and loving husband and father, who doted on his wife and his seven children and his several grandchildren. From all appearances, he lived happily until his dying day.

However, his mask of happiness hid a profound sadness, for in his heart he harbored a painful truth. There were doors, he came to realize, that could never be opened. Once shut, they would remain forever shut. No key, however crafted, could open them. He kept this sorrow locked away in a secret place. Hidden in the dungeon of the castle, behind a door that could only be opened with the master key he kept around his neck, was a vault that, once upon a time, held the Princess captive. Within, frozen inside a block of ice, he kept the Witch's head upon which remained the face of the Princess. And he would spend many an hour looking upon it and remembering how pretty was her face.

8—⊤

"The Keys to the Kingdom"
By
Susan Eager

Washington Monitor
Mexico Leans Left in Latest Election
By Charles Martinez
November 1, 2015

Mexico City, MX

Today marked the culmination of Mexico's most contested election in recent history when Jose Ruiz-Caldron was declared the next president. Ruiz-Caldron, a founding member of the relatively young National Socialist Party (*Partido Socialista Nacionalista*), has been elected by a wide majority to claim the country's highest office. The contest has been closely watched by many, particularly Mexico's northern neighbor, and is sure to have far-reaching implications for global politics.

Ruiz-Caldron is a former farmer from Chiapas, one of Mexico's poorest regions, which gained the spotlight for two weeks in 1994 when its Zapatista Army of National Liberation (EZLN) started a short-lived armed rebellion against Mexico's government. Ruiz-Caldron took part in the revolution as a teenager, but as his later speeches revealed, he realized that a small band of poor revolutionaries could not defeat an army. The now president-elect left the EZLN, taking up farming instead, and educated himself while working for equality and justice in his community.

Many Mexican journalists and politicians have compared Ruiz-Caldron to Abraham Lincoln, who was himself self-taught and a firm believer in equality. Some American pundits, however, have sought to remind the public that Lincoln's election precipitated a bloody and devastating war. These same pundits have criticized Ruiz-Caldron and his

131

policies, calling him a divisive figure who does not have the level-headedness to lead.

Despite warnings from their northern neighbors, Mexicans have embraced their new leader's humble beginnings, as well as his fiery speeches and political inexperience.

After founding the National Socialists Party (PSN) in 2008, Ruiz-Caldron traveled the country, giving speeches that emphasized fighting back against the economic oppression that he says many of his people struggle under due to exploitation by richer countries. His message gained popularity in the wake of the financial crises that hit the United States during the Second Great Depression less than a decade ago. With dwindling job prospects and a more strictly enforced immigration policy, the millions of dollars that had been sent home to Mexico by immigrant workers in the U.S. quickly vanished, practically crippling the Mexican economy. Combined with vast revisions of the North American Free Trade Agreement and the sinking value of the American dollar, the relationship between Mexico and the United States has quickly soured in the past few years.

Because Ruiz-Caldron's message is heavily leftist, it is expected that immense changes will be made to Mexico's government. One such change is a possible alliance with other socialist leaders in South America, as well as the Reformed Communist Russia (RCR). While the rumors of enormous financial support from Russia, Venezuela, Cuba, and other leftist countries have yet to be proved, a major alliance of this kind has surely put Washington on high alert.

Due to the unchecked escalation of oil prices over the past decade, both Venezuela and Russia have seen record profits while the U.S. economy has struggled. Both countries have expanded, Venezuela joining forces with nearby Colombia with Hugo Chavez as leader, and Russia creeping back into its former territories with excursions into Georgia, the Ukraine, and Serbia-Croatia. While the RCR has not officially declared control over these countries, it does seem to dictate their policy. An alliance between these countries and Mexico is almost certain, and this coalition is sure to have negative repercussions in the United States.

Supporters of Ruiz-Caldron took to the streets with the announcement of the election results, gathering in huge crowds, waving banners, and shooting off fireworks. The cheers of the crowd were so loud that the president-elect's speech was barely audible. Ruiz-Caldron did promise a new day for his people, "a day in which the economic tyranny of greedy capitalistic countries would be thrown off, as a starved mule throws off the plow when he can no longer bear the burden." Ruiz-Caldron continued, saying, "We must be as stubborn as that mule. We must stand firm in our resolve to reap the benefits of our own labor instead of submitting to a cruel, thieving master." This speech, like many others, was rife with such farm metaphors, which were part of his attraction to the common people, as well as his unkind words for the United States.

"He is one of us," one supporter said, waving a ripped banner containing Ruiz-Caldron's smiling face. "He knows how hard we work, how hard we struggle, with so little to show for it."

The celebration in Mexico City and many other cities and towns throughout the country is expected to last through the weekend. While Mexico enjoys its fiesta, it is certain that Washington will not be sharing in the celebration.

⊶

November 1, 2015
National Security Agency
Inter-Office Memo
Do Not Distribute

Effective immediately, regulation of the U.S.-Mexico border shall be severely tightened. The border fence shall be reinforced in all sectors to ensure security. Surveillance increases shall include high-definition cameras to cover every inch of the border wall, as well as new satellite surveillance technology to ensure complete coverage. Seismological equipment shall be installed in order to monitor for any underground excavation beneath the border wall. No breach in security should be possible.

The Coast Guard has been ordered to tighten its security in the Caribbean as well as the Pacific Coast. Patrols by air shall be quadrupled. All regions of the border, whether land, sea, or air, must be tightly monitored.

Check points between the U.S. and Mexico shall be heavily secured by the National Guard, effective immediately. Every person entering or leaving the country shall be photographed and fingerprinted. While this will create exceedingly long lines initially, it is expected that border crossings will decrease in frequency rapidly, and the procedure should become routine within the coming months.

While Mexico has yet to be declared a hostile territory by the United States government, its status has been escalated to High Watch status. We cannot afford to make any mistakes at this crucial time. Border security has become our Number One priority, above even homeland security and combating terrorism. We must remain vigilant. We must remain ready.

O—¬

March 20, 2016
Transcript of debriefing of Officer Zane Rodriguez by DEA Supervisor Charles Lakeland
26 minute mark

CL: So the incomes of the drug cartels are drying up?

ZR: Correct. The tightened border security has made it nearly impossible to move weight across the border. No tunnels, no boats, no aircraft, and they sure as hell can't drive it across anymore, with the National Guard standing watch. Even the mule herd has thinned out, since there aren't many jobs for illegals in the States now and the risks of getting caught are too high.

CL: Clarify these risks for us, if you will.

ZR: Well, any time you're muling narcotics, the first and most obvious risk is to physical health in the form of leakage or impaction. But as you know, Chuck, that doesn't stop too many of them, does it?

The second riskiest aspect is, of course, getting caught, and since the penalties in the U.S. have become stiffer, few want to risk imprisonment. La Migra doesn't round up the illegals and give them a free bus ride home anymore. That bus goes to prison now, and hell, even Mexico is better than el cárcel. But even prison isn't as scary to the mules as Los Serenos.

CL: You know my Spanish is terrible, Zane.

ZR: (*Chuckles*) "Los Serenos" roughly translates to "the Watchmen." This is their name for the National Guard. They're terrified of our new initiative when dealing with illegal border crossings. What the cartels are calling S.O.S.

CL: S.O.S.?

ZR: Shoot on sight.

CL: And how are the cartel bosses responding to the loss of income?

ZR: Well, for weeks they were pushing as much weight as possible at the border, hoping that most of it would get through based on the sheer quantities of the stuff. That failed miserably, as our overflowing evidence rooms show. Some of the cartels then joined forces, attempting to use their most trusted smugglers, guys they have bribed for years, men high up in our security and governance offices. But even this didn't work. Sentiments in the U.S. have changed, since Mexico is so politically distrusted at present. Everyone knows that it's unpatriotic to trust our brown brothers south of the border, now that they have virtually been declared terrorists by the media and government officials. (*Pauses, lets out a long sigh*) History will probably call this the "Brown Scare." (*Chuckles*)

CL: So has this tightened security finally won the War on Drugs?

ZR: (*Laughs*) Who knows? I will say this, these cartel guys aren't going to give up without trying every option. In fact, Pablo Patrón, head of the Bandidos Cartel, has been investing heavily in R&D.

CL: What in particular is he investing in?

ZR: Mierda, he's giving money to anyone who might uncover a key to unlock the border once again. He's writing checks to engineers, statisticians, scientists, transportation specialists, pilots, anyone and anything. I even heard that he was debating whether to build a giant catapult. (*Laughs*)

CL: We'll need the names of these individuals who are being paid to research alternate smuggling methods.

ZR: Sure. [List attached]

Excerpt of FBI Classified File 8LYUXT – Lem Ludaveko
Aliases: The March Hare, The Red Menace
DOB: 3-3-1959
Country of Origin: Latvia
Immigrated to the United States in 1983

Education: BS Physics, BS Chemistry at Moscow University
of Physics and Technology
          PhD in Biochemistry, The Ohio State University

Career: Assistant Professor at the University of Colorado
Professor at the University of Texas El Paso
Relocated to Juarez, Mexico, in 2009 to work for Farmasa
Internacional as lead
chemist in research pharmaceuticals. [Farmasa Internacional
is owned by Pablo
Patrón {see File 7YYLDF}].

Drugs designed by Lem Ludaveko at Farmasa Internacional
(FI), all of which are for sale in Mexico:

Antidepressents:
- Felizion – Failed FDA approval, never approved for
  sale in U.S.
- Tranquiloban – Recalled by FDA after 3 deaths

Selective Serotonin Reuptake Inhibitors:
- Dichamine – Recalled by FDA after several suicide
  attempts by users
- Firmezatine – Failed FDA approval, never approved
  for sale in U.S.

Criminal Record:

1983-1987: 2 arrests, Columbus, OH
          1 count of possession of illegal narcotics

1 count of possession of narcotics without a
prescription

1988-1995: 1 arrest, Boulder, CO
1 count of possession of controlled chemicals
without a permit

1996-2008: 2 arrests, El Paso, TX
1 count of possession of narcotics with intent to
distribute
1 count of possession of controlled explosives
without a permit

Organizations:

Immigrant Solidarity Network
International Society of Chemical Ecology
National Rifle Association
NORML
Republican Party
StoptheDrugWar.org
Strange Energy Organization

**Notes from Lem Ludaveko's abandoned apartment in
Juarez, Mexico**
Recovered May 19, 2016

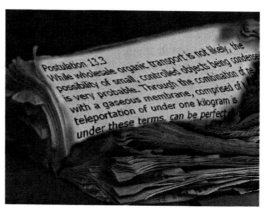

Postulation 13.3
While wholesale organic transport is not likely, the possibility of small, controlled objects being condensed is very probable. Through the combination of ... with a gaseous membrane, comprised of ... teleportation of under one kilogram is ... under these terms, can be perfect...

Excerpt from videotape of Lem Ludaveko's own testing process, left in Mexican apartment
Recovered May 19, 2016

A red-haired, disheveled Lem Ludaveko enters the screen and picks up a clipboard. Stationed next to him on the countertop is a silver box, of approximate dimensions 12 in. x 12 in. x 12 in. The box is hollow, having only four sides, which are marked with a small hole in the center of each. Ludaveko turns to the camera and begins.

"This is Trial 23, with object 8C, inert steel cube of 2.2 kilograms." Ludaveko inserts the object into the box and presses a recessed button on the top side of the cube. From the four holes a gas is emitted and the silver sides of the cube begin to glow. The power being conducted by the mechanism interacts with the gas inside it, causing a blinding flash. The gas dissipates rapidly and the box loses its glow. The object remains inside it, however.

Lem Ludaveko makes a notation on his clipboard and pushes his square-framed glasses up his hawklike nose. His upper lip twitches slightly as he forms his words. "Trial 23, failure."

The tape fades to black, then skips and squeals slightly as the next trial appears. Ludaveko again is positioned next to the silver box, and this time he slides a smaller object into his contraption. His white lab coat swings open just enough to allow the camera to see the tie-dyed t-shirt and jeans underneath. The scientist turns back to face the camera, picking up his clipboard and stating, "This is Trial 24 with object 8D, inert steel cube of .95 kilograms."

With the press of the button, the silver box begins to glow, and the gas is again emitted from the four small holes. The box charges up once more, interacting with the gas, and a bright flash again fills the lab. The gas clears, the box loses its glow, and Ludaveko's jaw drops as he stares at the empty cube. The clipboard slips from his hands and clatters against the tile floor as the scientist leans in for a closer look. His stunned face contracts into a smile as he mumbles, "Holy shit, it worked!"

The tape crackles and whizzes forward. Several more successful trials are presented, as well as many failures, so that Ludaveko is finally able to narrow down the parameters under which his teleportation device works. The final trial on the tape, Trial 107, opens with a noticeably cocky Ludaveko, sans clipboard and white jacket, pulling a lab mouse from a small wire cage.

"Trial 107, object 1X, live lab mouse, 1.2 ounces." His tone is distracted, his eyes red and weary, and his pupils are fully dilated. A small tic in his cheek bounces visibly, and he wipes the sweat from his brow as he slides the mouse into the box. Before he presses the button, he pulls a joint from behind his ears and lights it, inhaling slowly.

For the first time on the tape, Ludaveko offers the camera and his unseen audience information that is not directly related to the trials. Wiping his hand across his weary eyes, he begins. "I've been living in this lab, 24 hours a day, for over a month. I gave up my apartment when I noticed that I had acquired a tail. DEA, CIA, who knows? It's obvious that our actions have not gone unnoticed. Not surprising, given the impact of my invention. And my choice of associates."

Shaking his head and taking another puff, he changes course: "My machine already has numerous apparent applications beyond drug smuggling and will revolutionize the transportation industry, if the technology is allowed to spread beyond the cartels. But a successful test with a live subject will almost certainly have an immediate and world-shattering effect on mankind. Imagine human teleportation, speeding across thousands of miles in mere seconds." He pauses, his gaze far away. Putting the joint to his lips again, he takes a long drag, then silently chuckles. "And all because of this," he snorts, holding the joint up to the camera. "I guess this proves it – a junkie will do anything for his fix."

Ludaveko seems to notice that he is rambling, and wipes a palm across his right eye tiredly. "I'm not much for rhetoric, I guess." He smiles, then shakes his head, shouting, "Eff it, here comes the show!" With the press of a button, Trial 107 is under way. The box glows, the gas flows, and soon there is a flash.

Unlike the other times, this flash is accompanied by a loud pop as blood explodes from both sides of the hollow box. There is a scream, and the screen cuts to black. Here the tape ends.

Tape of wire worn by Agent Zane Rodriguez, undercover in the Bandidos Cartel
June 10, 2016

The tape is full of scratches as Agent Rodriguez's shirt rubs against the mic. Footsteps are heard, a door creaks open, and the footsteps change as the carpeted hall is exchanged for the laboratory's tile floor.

"Stinks in here," Zane mutters, and the mic easily picks up the voice of the husky man beside him.

"Si, hombre. Como el culo del burro." There is a hoarse chuckle from the left side, the side occupied by Pablo Patrón, whose thick voice sounds as if he were speaking from under piles of heavy flesh.

A man's high-pitched voice utters distractedly in the distance: "Welcome, gentlemen. Please do come in." The voice is accompanied by several scraping sounds as Lem Ludaveko fiddles around in the background.

Patrón coughs impatiently, and after several seconds he finally addresses the scientist. "Well, Lem, you loco bastard, what have you got that is so special you had to drag me down to this sucio lab in la media de la noche, eh?"

Ludaveko giggles and Zane questions, "Is your scientist high?"

Patrón mutters an obscenity under his breath. "Quizás, amigo. This hombre is always on something. Pero necesitamos un milagro, ¿no?"

Ludaveko's high voice sounds again, this time closer to the mic. "Señor Patrón, I'm about to give you the keys to the kingdom, my friend. This little box here is going to solve all your problems."

Patrón bursts out laughing. "This caja is your answer? How is this tiny thing gonna move weight north of the border?

You gonna train a bunch of rats to drag them over the fence? I swear, cabrón, if you have wasted my time and money – "

"Fear not," Lem interrupts with confidence. "Just watch carefully. Standing across the room you'll see Jorge, who is holding a syringe full of my … well, let's just call it my reward. He will place it in the silver box beside him, which is the same as the box here at my side. If you are ready, Jorge, place the syringe inside the box and press the button."

The tape is quiet, with the exception of a faint hissing sound that lasts for less than ten seconds. The wire picks up the sharp inhale of Agent Rodriguez, then his slow exhale. "Whoa."

Ludaveko continues, "As you can see, the syringe now resides in my cube, 100 feet away from its initial position. Gentlemen, you have just seen the world's first successful teleportation device in action. And now for my reward."

The mic picks up the muffled sounds of Lem as he pulls up his sleeve. There is the squeak and snap of rubber tubing, then a series of soft taps as the scientist flicks the syringe. The next sound the wire records is his contented sigh.

"Un milagro," Patrón says, almost in a whisper.

"Yes, a miracle," Lem giggles, "although one with specific operating parameters."

"Such as?" Zane asks.

"The device has a maximum range of 2,383 miles, and a maximum weight limit of one kilogram. And the object being transported cannot be alive, but that shouldn't matter in your business. I've built the prototype out of inexpensive, non-hazardous materials that can be easily purchased in order to cut down on production costs and time. They're small, as you've noted, and could even be sent by mail without arousing suspicion. We could have a thousand silver boxes by – "

"One kilo?" Patrón interrupts.

"Correct," Lem replies.

"How are we supposed to move weight like that, one key at a time?"

Lem responds calmly, "Thousands of boxes mean thousands of keys, at a rate of one key per 8.5 seconds."

Agent Zane exhales with force. "That's a lot of keys."

The wire can almost hear the smile that breaks across Patrón's face. "Looks like I'll need a big ass keychain."

Classified Memo
Maximum Security Clearance Necessary

To CIA Director Davidson
June 13, 2016

Recent intelligence indicates the possession of dangerous technology by criminal cartels in Northern Mexico. Consider this memo an authorization for the use of force in order to avert an impending crisis.

A team shall be established to seize the contents of the laboratory of Dr. Lem Ludaveko in Juarez, Mexico. Said contents are to be delivered to the National Security Agency immediately.

This operation is classified, and of the highest importance to the stability and security of this country. America will never back down in the face of a naked threat to the morals and values of its way of life. We must do what is needed to keep America secure.

With respect,
President S. Palin
Commander-in-Chief

⚰——

Text message found on the cell phone of CIA operative John Martinez to Alberto Gonzalez, cousin of Pablo Patrón.
July 16, 2016

JM: Circus is coming 2 town.
AG: ¿Verdad? When?
JM: SAT
AG: Lots of clowns packed in2 that car?
JM: At least a dozen.
AG: Looks like I'm buying tix 2 the Gr8est Sh0 on Earth…

⚰——

Telephone transcript of intercepted call between Pablo Patrón and General Humberto Alvarez
June 17, 2016

PP: Those northern gringos are serious. It's going down tomorrow. I've already cleaned out the laboratory, but it's obvious that we've got a ratón. It's certain that they ain't gonna stop coming after me. And if my business goes down, so do my … er … *contributions*, comprende?

HA: Entiendo, amigo. We've always appreciated your donations. That's why we've never shut you down.

PP: So, are you gonna help me ahora?

145

HA: Let me take this to my superiors. We don't let these pinche Americans push us around on our own soil no more. I'm sure El Presidente will have a plan when he hears about this.

PP: ¿El Presidente? What does he have to do with this? I just want you to get these gringos off my back. And to help me find the rat. Can't you just cut a deal with the Americans like always?

HA: There is no more "like always," amigo. The situation has changed. And I think this is just the opportunity we need. El Presidente will be very pleased.

PP: Wait –

Call Terminated.

⚿━

Helmet camera feed from Lieutenant Burt Kittson of raid on the Juarez laboratory of Lem Ludaveko
June 18, 2016

A black-clothed, helmeted ops team member, his Scorpion in his left hand, turns the laboratory doorknob with his right. The door swings open and the man slides into the dark opening, followed by the camera and the Lieutenant.

The night vision kicks in, outlining the surroundings in green and black. As the ops team files in, they begin opening cabinets and riffling through drawers, but it becomes immediately apparent that the laboratory has been abandoned. Lem Ludaveko and his silver boxes are nowhere to be found.

Without warning, the door to Ludaveko's bedroom bursts open to the camera's left. The Lieutenant quickly turns his head and the screen is filled with camouflaged Mexican

146

troops, their AK-47s blazing with light. This image persists for a split second only, as Lieutenant Kittson immediately drops to the ground and takes cover.

"Hit the deck!" he screams, cocking his gun and attempting to warn the team. For a moment the camera sees a man in camouflage drop, his face a bloody mess, as the ear-splitting sound of gunfire squeals over the tape and Kittson rapidly turns his head away to find the next target.

The remaining few minutes of footage are a blur. The laboratory is filled with fiery bursts as the special ops team stands off with the Mexican military. The camera catches the movements of the Lieutenant and his men, recording the deaths of those clumsy enough to fumble into someone's line of sight. The Mexican troops continue to tumble out from behind closed doors, filling the lab and quickly overpowering the black ops team.

The last image on the screen, after the Lieutenant stumbles, after he groans as a round hits his stomach, is the black-heeled boot of a soldier crushing the camera lens.

⚷

New York Tribune
Mexico Declares War on the United States
President Ruiz-Caldron vows to protect his border
June 20, 2016

President Ruiz-Caldron of Mexico declared war on the United States this morning without apparent warning. In a move that has sent shockwaves across the world, Ruiz-Caldron has closed the border with the United States and has expelled all U.S. citizens from his country.

Ruiz-Caldron insists that it was the United States who invaded his country over the weekend, and vows that he will protect the sovereignty of his people by any means necessary. His proof of the United States invasion, a video downloaded onto the Internet and sent to all major news networks, has become an instant sensation, crashing such sites as YouTube and The Smoking Gun, and even shutting down CNN.com with the deluge of hits.

The video has no sound and is only 1 minute and 32 seconds long. The camera pans across the corpses of a dozen black-clad, well-equipped men, then shifts to a table holding a line of American IDs, which Ruiz-Caldron insists belongs to the deceased.

While the White House vehemently denies any invasionary forces, it is keeping quiet on the identities of the bodies in the video. The President has said that she hopes for a peaceful solution soon, and has been attempting to reach Ruiz-Caldron herself to no avail.

President Ruiz-Caldron, while not taking calls from the White House, has been more than happy to speak to the press. "We have been ground beneath the boot of greedy America for too long. The U.S. feels it has the right to do what it will to countries it considers weaker than itself. America cannot stay strong forever, taking advantage of its allies, and robbing those who already have next to nothing. It is a nation of criminals, of thieves, who stole and cheated the very land upon which they founded their 'Home of the Brave.'

"Perhaps God will no longer bless America. Perhaps the home of the brave will become the home of the broken, as we take back the things they have stolen from us. Our land. Our water. Our dignity."

Although no official shots have been fired, both Mexico and America have elevated their threat levels to Red. Now there is an uneasy silence, as the eyes of the world turn with concern to the border.

⎯

Live Television Footage
The Evening News with Jefferson Lambert

July 4, 2016

A teary-eyed, slickly dressed newsman shoves away the stack of papers before him and looks directly into the camera and the terrified faces of the American public. "This afternoon, at 2 p.m. Eastern standard time, multiple explosions rocked every major city and strategic center in the United States."

The news feed switches to a slideshow of mayhem as the newscaster's voice continues. "The White House has been completely destroyed." A smoking ruin surrounded by fire trucks and ambulances fills the screen, then the picture changes to another pile of charred rubble, then another, as the newsman's voice cracks. "Capitol Hill, the Pentagon, the Supreme Court, Andrews Air force Base, West Point, and countless other locations have been hit. No accurate count has been completed on the casualties, but estimates are in the hundreds of thousands.

"The attack was well-planned and flawlessly executed. The trickles of information that we've been receiving say that thousands of devices were planted in every government building, state capitol, and military installation across the country. The remnants of the government and military have been slow to respond, saying only that they are investigating the possibility of – " The newscaster's voice breaks. " – of the widespread teleportation of explosive devices."

The newscaster's face returns, his skin nearly as pale as the sheet of paper he holds, his hand reflexively tightening, crumbling the paper into a ball. With a deep inhale, Lambert tries to get control of his features and stumblingly continues. "While none of the reports have been confirmed, it has been suggested that teleportation devices could have been planted at various locations without detection. If these devices were composed of materials that were not considered hazardous, they would not have set of any scanners and detection devices. Officials are not ruling out the possibility of these devices being sent through U.S. Postal Service as well."

Jefferson's eyes tighten as he continues to speak. "Mexico is claiming responsibility for the largest terrorist attack in history, along with its newly cemented allies: Russia, Venezuela-Columbia, Bolivia, Nicaragua, Panama, and Guatemala. President Ruiz-Caldron is calling this 'a great victory, which has all but won the war.' And with our crippled military and the possibility of new technology in the hands of our enemies, he may just be right."

⚷

Un anuncio de La Agencia de Turismo Nacional
12 de Septiembre 2016

¡Bienvenido a las tierras reconquistadas!

Visite bonita Florida, Tejas, Louisiana, California, Nevada, Nuevo México, Arizona, y otras ciudades de la nueva Republica Popular de México.

Si usted decide que disfruta los Estados Unidos anteriores y quiera permanecer allí, visite su Oficina Local de Relocación para más información …

 *(key icon divider)*

My key was the slang word for "kilogram ... "

When my old man and I were tossing around ideas for a
key story, we both came to the conclusion that "key" as in
"kilo" would be an interesting place to start. This brought us
to teleportation, and finally led me to Mexico overthrowing
the U.S. government and taking back the lands that had been
gradually taken from its people. The Re-Conquest of America
is an idea that has been kicked around by Chicanos for
decades, and I thought it was a fitting place to end my tale.
This is a soup of future-history and alternate-history, mixed
with my own extrapolations based on current events, and with
just a sprinkling of Spanish to give it spice. Thank you for
reading.

"Impossible Summer Snow"
By
Sheri McMurray

Based on the Bible account in Luke the second chapter,
"Impossible Summer Snow" tells this well-known story from a
whole new perspective. There are keys we hold in life that
unlock treasures we may not always see with our physical
eyes. It is the author's hope that even those who don't believe
in miracles may take pause and reflect on their possibility ...

⊙━┓

Old Ephraim, the sheepherder, gazed across the rolling
hills of the lands he was born in. The quiet pastures he never
ventured from his whole life. He listened to the summer
breeze whisper as it danced through the velvety green stalks
of grass. His wrinkled nose drank in the smells and sounds of
this his 102nd summer, and Old Ephraim remembered.

No snows had ever passed through these resplendent hills
in the late summers, close to the harvest season. Only warm
winds and chirping crickets, meadow larks, and tall feeding
grasses had ever graced these hills in the long hot summers
when a shepherd could lay out under the stars at night without
a blanket, and still be comfortable.

Except for the 90 years summer. The wonderful and
strange summer that this aged sheepherder kept close to his
faithfully beating heart. Old Ephraim always remembered the
night it snowed on these hills when it wasn't supposed to.

The bells on the shepherd dog's collar tinkled noisily as
the black and white Canaan went about the business of
keeping the sheep from going astray. This Canaan was the
descendent of several dedicated sheep dogs that worked hard
over the many years Ephraim had traversed these hills with
his flock. Ephraim closed his smoky olive-gray eyes and

155

remembered a night in deep summer when the sound of those bells had been drowned out by many voices.

As he lay back against the familiar pillow of grazing grass, with eyes still closed, he smiled as he subconsciously plucked a stalk of the vibrant grass and placed it between his teeth.

It wouldn't be long now. Ephraim knew it and the knowledge of it made a contented smile quietly grace his tanned, careworn face.

Ephraim lay back against the sweet-smelling grass of late summer, and as soon as he did his loving sheep dog came close and licked the aged sheepherder's coarse, whiskered face. The setting sun cast a radiant red glow across the clouds, which made the elderly shepherd warm clear through to his tired old bones.

After dinner prayers were said, after the flocks were herded in for the evening, after his good shepherd dog lay down beside him …

Old Ephraim lay under the twilight summer sky of his homeland, remembering. He closed his eyes and began to dream. Back over the years his heart wandered. Back 90 years in passing … and soon …

⚸━┳

Ephraim the young shepherd boy was sitting watching over his father's sheep.

The air had suddenly turned colder and he thought it odd. He wished for a cloak that he didn't have. He had not even a thin blanket to keep him warm. Just the fire left over from dinner preparations, and it was dying out.

Young Ephraim, the shepherd boy, watched his father peacefully sleeping and wished he was anywhere but on these hills in late summer with the flocks. He wished for a better dinner, a longer spring, new sandals, olive oil for the lamps.

He wished for the girl his parents promised, but that he was not allowed to see.

Ephraim was full of wishes that deep summer night. They all seemed to whisk away into nothingness, just as the last embers of the fire caught upon the wind and soon disappeared from his sight.

He poked at the dying glow of the fire with the end of his staff and thought of all the things his wise father had told him.

"Do not want for that which is beyond your reach."

"The days are coming when God will bless us, you will see."

"The girl we have promised you from the house of Asher is beautiful."

"Ephraim, have faith … "

Faith was hard to have when God had not spoken for over 400 years.

Young Ephraim sighed into the cool summer night. And his sigh became a wish and his wish became a prayer.

"Dear God of our Fathers, give me patience. I have so much in my heart to offer, but know not where to offer it. I have little possessions to give anyone, not to my family, or to the girl betrothed to me, or to even You, oh Gracious Giver. Forgive me for being anxious after everything, and for pestering You for much when much is not what I need."

He wondered how his father had endured all these years upon the hills with the sheep when the world was out there, vast and wide. He knew his father was a wise man and had never given him council that didn't prove out a just thing, but how was he to follow after his father when he was so impatient for the wisdom he needed?

Even so, Ephraim was to find that he was full of more wisdom than he ever dreamed he had. There was a gift waiting for him, a gift from a Gracious Giver. The Giver of Light would pass through time that late chilly summer eve, to give young Ephraim that gift personally.

That late summer's eve when the snowflakes came.

157

As he whispered his evening prayers, Ephraim the shepherd boy looked in wonder as he noticed his own breath linger then swirl as smoke upon the wind. He rose hesitantly to wake his father to ask if the sheep would be better tethered closer together as the night air increasingly became as frost.

And as he rose to place a hand on his father's shoulder, he saw them, curling gently down to the earth. Flakes of pure white frozen dew softly falling, one after another.

"What's this?" he whispered into the chilly night, "Surely, it is manna from Heaven."

Ephraim held out his hands, palms up, as the crystal flakes silently floated on the chill breezes and landed on them, the ground all around him fast becoming a soft blanket of pure white.

"Father ... " Ephraim stood transfixed and whispered, afraid to raise his voice, uncertain if he should reach out to stir the sleeping man.

His eyes followed the delicate flakes coming down from the heavens as the feeling of a strange presence began to overtake him.

Ephraim then traced those sparkling flakes up from whence they came, up into the pristine midnight blue of the cool summer evening sky. There were no clouds from which the snows came forth as in the winter. Yet here they tumbled, silent and wondrous like white feathers of frost without a cloud in the sky for them to emanate from. The sky was completely devoid of cloud or star.

Except for one bright and gleaming star.

Brighter and brighter the star became until Ephraim had to shield his eyes with his hand, then his whole arm. The brightness warmed him and he was suddenly glad, not frightened. Glad and warm, that is until the ground trembled and the quake began.

His father then awoke with a start. They both stood, arms shielding their eyes from the brightness, trembling alongside one another. And they both were so afraid! Nothing like this had ever happened before. Not to the boy too young to know of the world, or the man he called father with many years and experiences behind him.

Ephraim the young shepherd boy stood transfixed by the warming light, riveted to that one spot, unable to move. He felt the reassurance of his father's strong arm wrap around his shoulders. He was comforted by that strength. Love and comfort from his father, something he had felt many times throughout his childhood whenever he was afraid. And as the ground trembled, as the deep impossible summer snow fell around him, as the glow of the brightest star in the heavens bathed him in warmth, Ephraim looked over expecting to see his father standing by him with his arm around Ephraim's shoulders.

But the loving embrace he felt was not from his father, for Ephraim was mystified to find he stood there alone.

Just beyond where Ephraim stood hugged close as a loving embrace by the light radiating from the star, was Ephraim's father, on his knees in reverence before an incredible man. A man who glowed with the brightness of a thousand suns. A man with wings that stretched the entire breadth of the meadow where their sheep grazed. A man whose feet did not touch the ground. A man whose love wrapped around Ephraim, the shepherd boy's shoulders, with as much warmth and love as his very own father. A man whose eyes looked upon them both with tenderness and joy.

Much joy!

Exceeding joy!

Suddenly the entire night sky shimmered like the flower petals thrown into the air at a wedding and the air around him resonated into song. It was as if the entire earth trembled, filling his entire being with the glorious vibration of many thousands of voices. Such a multitude of voices it sounded like the rush of a hundred waterfalls cascading together. A stunning rainbow of colors danced before him, covering the heavens in the glowing luster of gemstones like the emeralds found in the breast plates of the temple priests.

The great gleaming winged man smiled and reassured them. "Don't be afraid!" he said. "I bring you good news that will bring great joy to all people. The King has been born this day in Bethlehem, the city of David!" As he spoke these words the air became like a great heart pulsating with jubilation.

"Go into Bethlehem," he announced in a voice more like a song than the spoken word, "and there you will find the babe in a stable at the inn."

Ephraim and his father had never before known such joy. Real, true, soul-filling joy. Such all-encompassing wonderful love that in the coming years, Ephraim would have a hard time not crying every time he retold this story to anyone who would give him ear.

Then just as suddenly as the snow began to fall, it receded. The winged man and the creatures who sang with him slowly faded from sight. He watched their faces smiling down at him and young Ephraim felt their warmth and power long after they were no longer in his sight. He could hear the delighted sobs of his father nearby, not a cry of fright or cowering submission, but that of a grateful man, as a man blinded his whole life who suddenly was made to see. The cries of a thankful man.

The chill breeze then whispered into young Ephraim's ear. It beckoned him to look down. And he obliged the breeze.

There, just at his feet beneath the still-white impossible summer snow, a thing strange and beautiful glowed.

Ephraim bent one knee to the snow and brushed the perfect white flakes from the object. As he did, he was amazed to find it was a key made of pure gold. He was just as amazed at this find as he was of the snowflakes and the winged man who brought such a strange message to shepherds on the hills this night.

"Ephraim," his father beckoned. "We must go now."

The boy quickly plucked the key from where it lay, noting it was warm to the touch and was strung on a golden chain. He placed it around his neck and scurried after his

father as he all but raced the sheep off the hillside to follow
the star into the city of David.

8—⊤

As the impossible snows subsided, Ephraim and his
father urged their flocks over the hills blanketed with the
silent, melting snow. They tethered the sheep in a shelter at
the outskirts, then made their way down into the valley where
the city of David was nestled.

They were drawn into the city by the one shining star,
which served as their compass. It guided them close to the inn
but not inside it. Instead the brilliant star hung suspended
directly over a rocky hill where a crude stable had been hued
out of the craggy gradient just behind the overcrowded
lodging.

There were many people of a lowly nature, simple people
like young Ephraim and his father, walking down the path
from the small stable where the innkeeper's animals were
kept. As each person silently passed, they smiled and gestured
back toward the stable, which was bathed in the light of the
one bright and lustrous star. Ephraim noticed their vesture was
not just a polite smile in passing, but that their faces radiated a
peace he had never seen before. Some, folk from tribes he had
never met, took him and his father and embraced them, then
without a word moved on.

Young Ephraim soon found himself standing in the
weathered entrance to the rudimentary stable, and what he
beheld there was a thing of wonder branded on his heart and
mind for the rest of his days.

A boy, much younger than Ephraim, whose clothes were
nothing but tattered rags, with not even a cloth tied upon his
feet to protect them from the harsh rocky ground, stood before
a man seated on the straw of the stable and a young woman
reclining beside the man with a newborn infant in her arms.
This little family was so poor they didn't have the means to

wrap the newborn in new linens, let alone afford a room at the inn. Instead they had their new baby wrapped in swaddling clothes.

Even in this squalor, the small boy played his drum as though he were playing for royalty: reverent, honorable, and with a look of true adoration on his dirty, tear-streaked little face. When he was finished, the man put a gentle hand upon the small boy's shoulder and in a loving tone said something to him. The young woman then smiled, and young Ephraim saw in her face not just a beauty, for she was comely to look upon, but a love for the drummer boy that radiated out from her very soul.

The small boy lovingly left the shabby old drum beside the cooing baby, then turned toward the door. The boy practically floated past Ephraim out of the lowly stable and into the clear crisp night.

It was then that Ephraim realized he and his father were the last visitors to enter the chilly stable that night. He was overcome by the dreary, foul-smelling habitat hardly fit for the animals that resided there, let alone the king that the lustrous winged man announced they would find there.

Ephraim remained on the threshold of the humble stable. It occurred to him as he beheld the couple and their baby that there were items resting all around them. Meager offerings perhaps, but gifts nonetheless. Among the soiled and broken offerings of those of poor and humble means who had visited before Ephraim and his father arrived, were three gilded boxes. Those golden boxes were of great value and obviously given by men of renown. Yet, even though the boxes were of much worth, it was odd that Ephraim didn't feel as though they were out of place among the rest of the gifts gathered before the couple and the baby.

Soon he uncertainly approached the little family resting on the harsh straw of the stable. Standing before the man, the young mother, and the babe, young Ephraim stammered with much disappointment evident in his voice, "I have nothing to give … "

As soon as the words passed from his lips, the strange and beautiful key that he had uncovered beneath the impossible summer snow began to glow again. Ephraim had forgotten about it dangling there around his neck from its golden chain, so overcome was he by the wondrous turmoil of events that flowed through this extraordinary summer's night with the arrival of the impossible summer snow.

His hand went to it and he clasped his fingers 'round the glowing item with excitement. At that moment, the baby laughed and the sweet tinkling sound of his laughter filled young Ephraim with a joy that penetrated him through to his inner being. And Ephraim couldn't help but laugh with the baby.

It was then Ephraim the shepherd boy knew the glowing item about his neck was meant for the babe all along. It was then that he lovingly took it from around his neck and held it out toward the tranquil family before him, and as soon as he did the three gilded boxes began to glow as well. It was then young Ephraim knew the Gracious Giver had a plan for his life all along and had bestowed him with this gift. A key, which in turn unlocked truth, a truth that he would always give back to others.

Without thinking, young Ephraim placed the glowing key into the ornate hasp of the first gilded box, then the fixtures of the next two, until each box lay open, glistening exquisitely in front of the company assembled together in the stable that night.

Gold, frankincense, and myrrh gleamed of their own accord, obviously worth much in the viewpoint of the earthly eye. But the truth then occurred to Ephraim: they were also symbols of the worth of life, the fragrance of peace, and the promise of faith. This wondrous key from the heart of the Gracious Giver not only unlocked these beautiful boxes, but also the true reason for our existence.

"You have brought us the key that unlocks the means by which we will survive and protect our son until he grows to manhood. Without this key, these three offerings from the

Magi would have been rendered useless." The man then placed his warm, strong hand upon young Ephraim's shoulder and spoke in a gentle tone, just as he had to the drummer boy and young Ephraim felt what the drummer boy had felt.

He gained a quiet tranquil knowledge he would carry with him the rest of his days.

The baby laughed again, and when he did all who were gathered around him were filled with not only jubilation, but a sobering truth. That truth is that although life is hard and at times it may even seem like this life is too overwhelming, even in the face of all that, there is the promise that miracles will happen.

Then young Ephraim bent to the baby and kissed his delicate pink cheek and an amazing thing happened. Something Ephraim had a hard time describing as he retold this story as the years went by. It was as if the light from the star flooded the stable at that very instant, as a flash of lightning. It was suddenly there and gone, but in that instant young Ephraim felt every good thing, every peaceful moment, every peal of laughter, uttered by every human being down through the ages of time. That joy overpowered him and everyone standing within the rugged stone walls of that cramped, degraded stable.

The young mother smiled at him and Ephraim saw in her eyes more wisdom than she had years. She quietly said the words he'd heard his father say so many times he could not count, but now coming from her lips they had renewed truth and meaning. Because on the night of the impossible summer snow, Ephraim the shepherd boy knew he had touched the face of Adonai.

"Ephraim, El àåôï, The Key Giver … have faith," she whispered.

Ephraim expressed his thanks to her with a warm, knowing smile.

Ephraim, the shepherd boy, son of a shepherd, The Key Giver, carried forth all he had experienced that night, to every ear poised to listen, for the rest of his days. He did this dutifully, often to ridicule, sometimes to wrath, but faithfully his entire life. He aptly called it the good news.

He knew the young mother and he would someday meet again. When they did, he knew it would be a tender night like this.

In his 102nd year, under the glittering stars of this peaceful summer night, Old Ephraim lay upon the sweet grassy hillside with his flocks and smiled in his sleep.

Once again the young mother's voice echoed to Ephraim from the site of the nativity ...

"Have faith ... "

Ephraim came back to the sweet green meadow, where the impossible summer snow had fallen 90 years ago, with an indelible knowledge. He came there not to watch the sheep, reminisce over memories long passed, or to nod and dream as the old men of the village often did. Instead on this evening he came there, secure in the knowledge that this was exactly the place God wanted him to be.

For this was the evening the impossible summer snow would fall around him once again.

This was the night the man who glowed as a thousand suns, who placed the key to unlock the treasure of life at a young shepherd boy's feet, the man with the wings that stretched the breadth of the meadow, would wrap those golden radiant wings around Ephraim just as he had that summer so long ago.

She was there too, as the sparkling impossible snowflakes began to fall. She and the Gracious Giver as well. This night the brilliant winged messengers sent to proclaim the good news to lowly shepherds tending their flocks on the hills overlooking that little town nestled in the hills of his homeland, would visit El àåôï, the Key Giver, one last time.

They smiled in greeting, just as they did a lifetime ago when he was but a boy and she was young and hope was invincible. His heart then swelled with that same remarkable joy. The snows enveloped him and the wings wrapped warmly around his shoulders.

The Gracious Giver held out his hand and Ephraim instinctively raised his to meet it. When he did, the Gracious Giver laid the glowing golden key in the wrinkled palm of the old shepherd, and as the key touched Ephraim's skin, the calluses melted away. His skin became young, soft, and supple once more, just as it was the night he met the babe in the stable at the inn.

The young mother smiled at Ephraim, just as she had that night long before. Then the winged man and the Gracious Giver swept him off his feet and Ephraim hovered with them as a feather, floating within the frozen white dew of uncountable brilliant glistening snowflakes.

"Ephraim, El àåôï, the Key Giver, The Key is yours forever now," Ephraim heard the lustrous winged man say, his voice warm and soothing as a song. "Take it and we will walk the rest of the way together."

"Welcome to the Crossroads"
By
D.G. McMurry Jr.

*My key is about perspective. I have always wanted to tell
a story about how we view our world and how it affects our
lives, but in such a way that it was a tangible thing to the
main character. So, I had the idea of the protagonist
wandering into a bar that wasn't quite what it seemed from
the outside. During one of our weekly talks with the group,
someone mentioned how they enjoyed when characters from
one story made a cameo in another story. One idea meshed
with the other, and the Crossroads Inn was born. If you pay
really close attention, you might even catch my "tip of the
hat" to my fellow authors. I hope you enjoy the story.*

⚷—

Distant thunder echoed down the empty city street, as the
rainstorm moved out of the valley and into the surrounding
mountains, a few hours before midnight. Daneville was small
as municipalities go; only thirty or forty thousand people. The
traffic on the main highway through town usually settled
around eight-thirty as the shops along main street closed for
the night.

Tony Marcus thought it appropriate that it had chosen to
rain that evening; he'd lost his job, then his girlfriend, and the
short but violent downpour had been the perfect capper for an
imperfect day.

Tony dragged his feet down the rain-slicked sidewalk,
scuffing his good work shoes. He never really fit in with the
office crowd; it was amazing to him that two years on the
college fencing team did little to prepare him for the verbal
thrust and parry his former job required of him. In fact, he
mused, the people he had worked with probably wouldn't

169

even realize he was gone.

Earlier he had slipped the knot of his tie loosely around his neck, and opened the top button of his collar. One shirt tail protruded from his permanent press slacks, his disheveled appearance reflecting the mood of his day.

Tony had taken to wandering the streets of the city in which he lived just after sundown, and prior to the sky opening up and dumping on him also.

As he neared the end of yet another street, the clouds parted slightly, allowing a few stars to peek timidly among the remaining wisps of the rolling thunderheads. The receding storm left behind a chilled mid-night breeze.

Tony realized he had wandered to the northern edge of town. The temperature was dropping; somewhere in his wanderlust he had shed his coat, and now his soaked clothing was only enhancing the passing breeze.

The sidewalk abruptly ended at the newer buildings of the street, but it left him pointed at the old tavern that existed on the city's fringes. In the years that Tony had lived in the city, he had never seen the place occupied, and yet on this particularly dark and stormy night, light filtered through the slits of the drawn shutters on the face of the building.

Caving in to human curiosity and figuring nothing else could possibly happen to him that hadn't already, Tony approached the dilapidated structure. He stepped upon the decrepit stairs, slowly testing each. Each groaned under the pressure of his weight, but surprisingly remained intact.

Tony's gaze rested upon the oversized oaken double doors that led into the tavern. The doors, when they were made, must have been quite remarkable, each covered with intricate carvings of vines and tree limbs. Situated in the center of each door was what was once a beautiful stained glass window that held a golden crown and crossed swords, but was now so filthy that from a distance they could have easily been mistaken for part of the wood.

Shoved in the seam between the glass and the wood was a parchment-colored plastic sign that read "Help Wanted."

Tentatively Tony's right hand reached out to grasp the ornamental handle; he pressed his shoulder against the door, and leaned into the tavern.

A friendly glow filled the great room of the edifice, and its warmth rushed over him. A popping, cracking fire filled the stone hearth on the east side of the room, and along the back wall ran the most elaborate bar Tony had seen in his short twenty-five years (not that he was any kind of expert). Its deep cherry wood had been shined to a reflective perfection, and gold and silver inlays bounced the flickering firelight around the room.

Treated pine planking crossed the room north to south forming the floor, each aligned as if to invite one from the entryway and directly to the bar. Chandeliers lit the rest of the room with a soft, diffused light that seemed to enhance the firelight, without making the room shadowed around the tables that filled the space between the front doors and the bar.

Behind the wood rail of the bar and extending eight feet above the floor, was a shelf that contained every variation of a glass bottle Tony could have ever imagined, filled with color after color of what he assumed were exotic intoxicants. Leaning at the far edge of the shelf stood a rolling ladder, not unlike those found in the local college's library.

"Are you comin' in, or are you gonna let all my heat out?" a gruff voice grumbled from behind the bar.

"Sorry," Tony replied to the disembodied voice, and quickly closed the door behind him. "Excuse me," he called, "are you closed?"

"Closed?" the voice chuckled. "'Course not, I'm jus' openin' for business. Welcome to the Crossroads."

The owner of the voice abruptly appeared from his hiding place behind the cherry wood rail. The crotchety voice emanated from a rather stocky man about five and a half feet tall. His crusty demeanor was only enhanced by the thick woolen black beard upon his face and the heavy bushy eyebrows.

"You here 'bout the job?" he grunted as he finished

171

wiping the sparkling glass he held in his hands, and set it upon the dark wood surface.

"No, no, not really," Tony stammered. "Just looking for a place to drown my sorrows, I guess."

"Tough one today, huh?" the Innkeeper said as he continued polishing his glasses.

"My father had a saying: *You can polish a road apple all you want, but in the end all you have is a horse turd,* and that's what this day has been."

"Well I s'pect this is as good a place, if not better, than any, to lose yourself for a while. You jus' well pull up a seat, the regulars will be showin' up soon." The bartender motioned to soft padded leather stool. "What's your pleasure? A slight euphoria or total amnesia?"

"Let's start with euphoria," Tony chuckled, "and we'll see where it goes from there."

"You're the boss." The bartender reached behind him, grabbed an amber-colored liquid that he delicately poured into the glass on the bar, and slid it within Tony's reach.

"There ya go. Want to run a tab or pay as you go?"

Tony reached into his back pocket and retrieved his wallet. He grabbed out all the cash he had and slid it back across to the bartender and tossed the empty wallet on the bar top.

"Let's see how far that'll take me," Tony responded.

"Sure 'nuff … " The bartender eyed his only customer.

"Anthony Marcus," he supplied. "Just call me Tony."

"Sure 'nuff, Tony. I'll let you know if you start runnin' low," the barkeep said, his voice warming to Tony.

"Thanks … "

"Myakel Strongaxe," the bartender smiled. "Myke will do."

"Thanks, Myke." Tony sipped his first drink of the night. "So I haven't noticed your place before."

"No, I havin' seen ya before. You probably didna need my services before now," Myke replied, polishing a glass.

"Maybe you can just tell me the meaning of life." Tony

took a sip of his drink.

"That's easy," Myke remarked. "Life is much like this drink. Bitter and sweet, and only the right combination of these ingredients together can make the whole worth drinkin' – or livin'."

"Well between women woes and work, life sure hasn't seemed to have much meaning today."

"Ah, women. I knew a great woman once. Holly. Or was it Susan? You know, maybe it was Sally. Anyway, I understand whatcha mean."

Tony's eyes strayed up to the back of the bar. Up close the names on the bottles were almost as fascinating as the colors contained within. His eyes scanned the shelves, labels like *Purple Moon, Whigham's Best Ale, Sherri's Sherry, Leila's Legal Libations, Valin's Vitamin Vitalis, Steve's Finest Bordeaux,* and a particularly lethal-looking bottle, simply labeled *esr960*, jumped out at him.

Most bars he had been in had a mirror behind the center of the work area, but here was a battle axe of immense proportion. The axe obviously wasn't just a show piece but something that had been used and also well cared for. The axe was framed by the multitudes of colored bottles. Mounted to the wall was a cradle in which the two-headed battle axe rested – the grips told of its years of use. The age of the metal head was obvious, but the quicksilver edges also showed that it was lovingly honed to a rapier edge by its owner.

"What's the story with the axe?" Tony asked, signaling for another round.

"It keeps the peace," Myke responded, laying another drink on the bar.

"Seems quiet enough," Tony commented, scanning the empty room.

"Give it an hour or so, it'll fill in. Trust me." Myke smiled, patted the head of the axe, and started putting glasses on the shelf behind him.

Tony had nursed about six drinks or so; he had lost count around the third drink so he wasn't absolutely sure. He glanced down at his watch. It had stopped around nine-thirty. *That figures,* he thought, *no job, no girlfriend, dead battery.*

A gust of wind blew the door open and it appeared to Tony that the storm had resumed its fury outside once again. Lightning flashed in the dark sky.

An old man in long a gray cloak and a tall, oddly pointed hat came through the door with the gust, closely followed by a rather regal-looking man dressed in some kind of greenish clothing and a cloak of heavy dark-green cloth that Tony took to be some kind of hunting outfit.

The older of the two men smoothed water from his gray-white beard with one hand and clasped a wooden staff in the other, making Tony think he looked like a storybook wizard. The two men shook the water from their cloaks, hung them to dry by the doorway, and made their way to a corner table by the fire and settled in.

The younger man in the hunting clothes sat with his back to the wall. They both removed elaborately carved pipes within the folds of their clothing and lit up. The wizard began blowing intricate smoke rings, bringing a smile to the hunter's lips, as his eyes scanned the room. The hunter's gaze fell on Tony and he made a slight acknowledging nod, then finished looking the room over. He then spoke to Myke as he came over to their table.

Myke moved back behind the bar and retrieved three pewter mugs and a pitcher of some dark liquid and returned to the table. As Myke set the drinks before his new customers, someone else entered. The new arrival stood three or four feet tall, and was dressed similarly to the hunter that had proceeded him, and from Tony's viewpoint looked no more than a child of eight or ten.

The kid smiled as he passed Tony at the bar, his blue eyes

174

piercing Tony's soul for a moment. As the kid passed him, Tony realized that the youngster wasn't wearing any shoes and that he had the biggest, hairiest feet he had ever seen. Tony turned back to the bar and noticed Myke had returned and refilled his glass.

"What's with the kid?"

"That *kid* is older than you are," Myke said. "This is one of the few places the three of them can still get together anymore." Myke went back to his glass cleaning.

Tony glanced at the trio again. The three of them were laughing at some unheard tale, as they each drew smoke from their pipes, different colored smoke rings dancing above their heads.

I didn't realize the Renaissance fair was in town already, Tony thought as the storm banged the door open again.

Lighting flashed momentarily, silhouetting the four men in the doorway. They made their way into the room to one of the central tables and sat. The four men were similarly dressed, with the exception of their shirt colors: two wore blue, one a goldish color that kept changing depending on the lighting, and one in red. They each wore black pants that came just below the knee, and highly shined black boots.

Myke hurried over to the table, took their orders, and came back to the bar and started pouring drinks. As he finished, the doors swung inward again, admitting more customers: one rather huge man (tall and wide) of Turkish decent, one rather rakish-looking Spanish man, and a smaller and balding Sicilian. Again, they all appeared dressed for the Renaissance fair or something similar.

The balding Sicilian, who appeared to be the leader of this particular group, hollered at Myke to get his attention. Myke turned to Tony.

"Hey Tony, do me a favor and give those four these drinks," Myke said, pointing at the dressed-alike men.

"Sure Myke," Tony said, taking the tray from him and moving over to the men.

"So I said to her, I work in space, but I'm from Iowa," the

handsome guy in the goldish shirt said as Tony neared the table.

One of the men in blue, who seemed to be older and had a rather dour expression, just rolled his eyes.

"Fascinating," the taller man in blue with upswept eyebrows stated.

"Really, that line worked, captin?" the man in red shirt commented with a bit of Scottish brogue.

"Like a charm. It's timeless," the captain replied, a cocky grin on his face.

"The only way that will be timeless is if you travel back in time and use it," the older, cranky man in the blue shirt remarked.

"Gentlemen," Tony set his tray on the table. "Your drinks. I'm sorry I don't know whose is whose."

"Mine's the green one," the Scotsman said, reaching for the indicated drink.

"The water is my order," the taller of the men in blue quietly stated, reaching for the frost-covered glass.

"Which one's yours, Doc?" Tony asked the older gentleman at the table.

"How did you know I was a physician?" Doc asked, pointing to one of the remaining drinks.

"Something in you demeanor reminded me of an old country sawbones I knew when I was a kid," Tony replied, setting the final drink in front of the captain.

To this, the captain and the Scotsman both began to laugh, while the quieter man just lifted his eyebrow, and the Doc scowled.

"You gentlemen don't hesitate to ask if you need anything else," Tony said, picking up the tray. As he passed the man with the upswept eyebrows, he commented, "I didn't realize there was a convention in town. Good job on the ears, by the way." This drew a laugh from the Doc as well.

"The universe is seldom as we see it," the man remarked to Tony with a lift of his right eyebrow.

"Hey, Tony," Myke greeted, as Tony returned the tray to

the bar, and Myke continued to fix drinks for his customers.

"So Myke, do you get a lot of conventions here?"

"Conventions?" Myke asked, not looking up from his work. "I forgot! The doctors' convention is tonight!"

"A doctors' convention?" Tony was surprised that a group of doctors would want to come here for a convention, considering the clientele Tony had seen so far.

"Not 'a' doctor's convention, there's only ten of them, but they are a rowdy group when they all get together." Myke paused, and then, making a decision, looked Tony in the eye. "I know you weren't necessarily looking for a job, but it's shaping up to be a busy night. Would you mind giving me a hand?"

"Sure," Tony replied, glancing at his watch out of habit. It had moved five minutes since he looked the last time.

I guess I need to take this thing in and have it checked tomorrow, Tony thought, then commented to Myke; "I didn't realize there were so many conventions in town."

"Wha?" Myke asked, and then the door banged open yet again, admitting a white bearded old man in brown robes, and a youth wearing a baggy white tunic and tan leggings with boots.

"Could you take these drinks to the three in the corner?" Myke pointed to the Turk, the Spaniard, and the Sicilian. "I need to keep an eye on this guy, he can be a bit cranky and people who tick him off tend to lose arms."

Tony grabbed the drinks and approached the table.

"It's inconceivable," the balding Sicilian was telling the other two. "The Princess ... " The balding guy shushed the other two as Tony set down the drinks.

"I don't think you know what that word means," the roguish Spaniard with the mustache said.

"You gentlemen need anything else?" Tony inquired.

"No, my good man." The bald man made a motion to swish Tony away. "If you don't mind, my colleagues and I have business. Private business."

As the night moved on, Tony helped Myke keep up with

the steady flow of people in and out of The Crossroads. Tony met people of all shapes and sizes, some dressed more bizarrely as the night progressed. There were a few incidents that made Tony question what he saw, but he just chalked it up to the lateness of the hour and the rough day he had.

Tony stole a glance at his watch. It showed a little past ten.

What is with this thing? Tony thought. *So much for high-quality workmanship.*

Tony was still contemplating his malfunctioning timepiece when he turned with a tray full of drinks in his hands and ran headlong into one of the meanest-looking beings he had ever seen. The guy was a good eighteen inches taller than Tony and covered with black and silver armor, a gold metallic sash ran across his chest, and his boots had sharp metal spikes sticking up out of them.

Tony looked up into his opponent's face. A ridge of bone sat above the warrior's eyebrows and the fellow's face drew back in a snarl, his crooked yellowed teeth clenched tight.

"Sorry," Tony started.

With a deep rumble from his chest, the recipient of the spilled drink grabbed Tony by his tie and lifted his feet from the floor. The tray and drinks clattered to the floor.

"It's not too smart to wear one of these in a bar fight," the huge and really ticked off warrior said in a deep gravelly voice as he lifted Tony a bit higher by his tie.

"I wasn't intending on getting into a bar fight ... " Tony managed to croak. Though he considered himself in pretty good shape, despite having spent the last few years behind a desk since graduating college, Tony realized he was little match for the giant warrior that held him like a rag doll.

An arrow whizzed between the faces of the two men and *thunked* into the wall by the bar, cutting the tie neatly in half and dropping Tony to the floor and onto his backside.

The former contents of Tony's tray covered the spot in which he landed, part of which was a blue fluid that smelled like year-old Easter eggs, inside a pair of gym socks, under a chicken coop.

The big warrior made to retrieve Tony from his landing spot. A thunder-like clap echoed across the inn, causing everyone to stop what they were doing and turn toward the bar.

"That'll be enough," Myke said, resting his hand on the handle of his axe, which he had used to make the sound that had gathered everyone's attention.

The big warrior grunted and sounded like he was gagging at the barkeep. It wasn't until Tony heard "prune juice" that he realized the warrior was ordering in some form of language. The warrior's disposition still looked quite menacing, but for all Tony knew, the warrior could have been happy. But when the big man got his order of some live wiggling mass in a gelatin base, Tony figured between that and the prune juice, maybe the man who almost choked him to death was just having trouble in the restroom department.

A hand extended into Tony's eyesight, offering him a lift up, which Tony gratefully accepted. The man before him held a bow in his left hand and grasped Tony with his right.

"Thanks," Tony commented, nodding to the archer.

"No problem," the archer smiled, and retrieved his arrow from the wall.

"Nice shooting, Rob," Myke commented from behind the bar, as the archer waved and disappeared back into the crowd, which was slowly dispersing back to their seats now that the excitement was over.

"Tony," Myke said after returning his peacekeeper back to the wall where it belonged, "I have a change of clothes in the back, maybe you should use them ... "

Tony made a feeble attempt at cleaning off his clothes, then nodded and disappeared into the back room.

After a few minutes, Tony returned to the bar wearing buckskin breeches, leather boots, and a tunic.

"I feel like I should be riding the plains with a masked stranger," Tony commented to Myke. "So, Myke, tell me what's really going on here. These guys aren't from some convention or fair."

Myke squinted his left eye and examined Tony with his right eye, as if looking at him for the first time. Then cleared his throat.

"It's kind of hard to explain. The guy with the pointy ears tried once, but he lost me somewhere between inter-dimensional rifts and space-time dilations. Suffice to say what's fiction to you may well be someone else's reality. It is all in how each of us perceives his surroundings. Some, like the gentleman with the pointy ears, perceive more of their surroundings than others."

"So I am right, there is more to this Inn than just a little out of the way getaway," Tony said, with a look of *eureka* on his face.

"I noticed you kept glancing at your watch throughout the evening. Haven't you noticed that time runs a little differently between these walls?" Myke replied.

"I just assumed something was wrong with my watch." Tony glanced at his watch. The crystal was shattered from his brief encounter with the angry warrior, and the watch had truly stopped, showing the time as a little past midnight.

"Only in the sense that it can't keep time, where time really has no meaning. That's not what's really important here. Stopping at The Crossroads, everyone, in every time, dimension, or space, is seeking something – peace, adventure, companionship, camaraderie – and here for a few hours, that's possible, if however brief. And I do what I can to make them happy, and keep the peace."

⊖━⊤

After their little talk, Tony began to notice more about his surroundings and the beings that currently inhabited The Crossroads. One in particular was an immense being that at first glance Tony assumed him to be a guy dressed in a big green scale suit, when in fact he was just a big green scaly guy. Big green and scaly had risen angrily from the table, but surprisingly it was the young man who sat with him that was first to attack the offender. Using some unidentified power, the youngster flung the offender against the far wall where he sagged to the floor.

"What was that all about?" Tony asked Myke, stunned.

"The big green guy takes offense to being called a pervert, and his apprentice doesn't take it well either," Myke responded.

The rest of the evening was a blur of faces and drink orders, and Tony couldn't remember being happier. It seemed to him that all of his problems didn't amount to much compared to the vastness of the universe he saw within the walls of this out-of-the-way inn that he had stumbled into hours, days, weeks ago. Tony wasn't even sure anymore how long it had been; time had stood still here for him as well. However, the crowd thinned out and eventually Myke and Tony stood in the Inn alone.

"Storm's passin'," Myke said, putting a chair on the table. "It'll be a beautiful day in a few hours."

"So this happens every night?" Tony helped Myke pick up the chairs.

"Pretty much," Myke replied, still cleaning.

"I have so many questions, but I guess the one bugging me the most is how did you wind up with all of this?" Tony asked, sweeping his arm to encompass the great room of the Inn.

Stopping for a moment in his cleaning, Myke turned to Tony, and after giving it some thought, replied.

"I was like you," he said simply.

Tony gave him a skeptical look.

"Okay, not exactly like you," Myke chuckled, and started cleaning again. "I lost my way once, not sure where to go or what to do and I found my way here, and it's treated me pretty well all my life since. But I'm gettin' too old to break up bar fights every night."

"So the help wanted sign." Tony paused. "I'd like to stay

and help you."

"Tony," Myke stopped again to face the youngster, "you're a good man, but I wasn't lookin' for help, I'm lookin' for a replacement. I thought when I first saw you, you were the man, and you did great this evenin', but I'm not so sure."

"But … " Tony protested.

"No, hear me out." Myke held up his hand. "You're at a crossroad in life. Like I tried to explain earlier, your perspective is the key to your universe."

Tony thought back to their conversation earlier, and the comment by the guy with the pointy ears. *What if he had spent most of his life unaware of what was truly going on around him?* Tony had been so involved in earning a living and managing his life, maybe he forgot how to really live it. Tonight was the first time he really felt a part of something vastly bigger than his own corner of the universe.

"The world to you won't be the same," Myke continued, "and I think it would be better if you experienced that world through fresh eyes."

"I would really like to stay, Myke," Tony softly replied, afraid that he would lose what he had discovered here if he left.

"I know," Myke sighed. "Help me finish cleanin' up a bit and I will sleep on it, okay?"

"Sure, Myke," Tony responded, trying to keep the disappointment from clouding his voice.

⚷

Sunlight filtered through the crack in the shutter, shining right into Tony's left eye. The wooden surface under his cheek threw him for a moment, making him wonder where he was, and why he wasn't in his own bed. He woke and rubbed his face as he looked around. His memories of the previous night came flooding back. The Inn was just as he remembered, except a fine layer of dust had settled over

182

everything. The tables and the chairs that filled the Inn were covered with white cloth.

The fireplace stood cold and empty. The back was covered with black stains; no firewood or ashes stood in the hearth. It appeared the Inn had been deserted for months, if not years.

"Myke?" Tony's voice echoed in the confines of the great room. Tony's senses came crashing to reality.

"It was all a dream, wasn't it?" he whispered to himself.

Tony stood up. The bar stood as it had the night before, except the shelves were bare and the holder for Myke's peacekeeper stood empty.

Tony had only cried twice in his adult life, once when his mother had passed and a few years later when he lost his father. Now the emotion welled up in his throat and threatened to overwhelm him. Tears stood at the corners of his eyes.

"No," Tony choked the word from his throat.

"No," he said, again, more firmly, "I refuse to believe this."

Tony turned back to the table he had been sleeping on; it was bright and shiny, as if it were just cleaned. In fact, he remembered, he cleaned it just before he passed into sleep. In the center of the table stood a back pack and some other stuff wrapped in furs and oilskins. Lying on top of the pile was a note:

If you are reading this (and obviously you are) then you remember what I told you about the key to the universe.

Here's a few things to help you on your journey. Experience what you have learned and what you have yet to learn. When you are truly ready, the job will be waiting for you.

Your friend, Myakel Strongaxe,
Myke

Tony grabbed the pack and stuffed the note in it, then gathered the other items from the table and went to the door, but it wasn't quite the same door he entered another lifetime ago. The beautifully inlaid oak doors were rubbed and oiled to a deep, dark luster; the stained glass sparked as light struck its surface.

The dawn glinted off the dew covering the forest flora, like so many twinkling stars. The air was crisp and clean; the fresh rain had left a washed scent of adventure in the air. The new world stretched before him, a world of promise, a world that waited his first steps in anticipation.

Tony knelt on the landing before the Inn doors and unwrapped the oil cloth. Shielded within the folds was a magnificent sword. The blade shimmered in the morning light, almost as if it glowed with an inner fire in its scrolled edging. The second wrapping held a belt and scabbard as lovingly crafted as the sword they were meant to bear.

Tony placed the sword reverently back on the oil skin and bound the scabbard with the belt to his hip. As he stood, Tony raised the sword to greet the rising sun, and its finely honed edge glowed orange in the morning light.

Someone named Tony would be unlikely to wield such a weapon, he pondered as he swung the steel in ever-increasing arcs, feeling as though the blade were an extension of himself. *Marcus is a good, strong name*, he decided as the kaleidoscope of his blade sliced through the morning air.

Firesword, Marcus smiled to himself, concluding to leave "Tony" behind. *Marcus Firesword,* he thought as he sheathed the weapon and gathered up the rest of his equipment and stepped away from the Inn and onto the muddy path that led between the forest's trees, over the horizon.

The forest sounds and smells assaulted Marcus as he trod up the hill. Eventually he reached the peak in the path; before him he saw a green valley and a small village, down where the trail ultimately led.

Looking back over his shoulder, he saw the faint outlines

of the Crossroads Inn, against the vast forest of autumn colors, smoke rising from its chimney as its proprietor started his day.

Marcus smiled. Someday he would return to the Inn, but for now, he turned toward the horizon and into his first of many adventures.

⚷

About the Authors

Christopher J. Valin

Christopher J. Valin is a writer, artist, historian, and high school social studies teacher living in the Los Angeles area with his family. He has been writing in many forms since he was a small child, including short stories, comic books, and screenplays. Christopher was the winner of Week 3 of the FanLib.com Kirk vs. Picard screenwriting contest, and his other screenplays and teleplays have won or placed in several other competitions, including the Scriptwriters' Network Producers Outreach Program, the Nicholl Fellowship, the Chesterfield Fellowship, the Fade In Competition, and Scriptapalooza. He is currently finishing up his master's degree in military history with a concentration on the American Revolution and hopes to one day publish a book about his 5x great-grandfather, Sir Charles Douglas, who played a major part in that war.

187

Eugene Ramos

Eugene Ramos is a recent graduate of Columbia University's Film Division. He's won writing contests for the sci-fi TV shows *Star Trek*, *Painkiller Jane*, and *Battlestar Galactica*. Interestingly, as an undergrad, he majored in British Literature and Poetry of the 1500s. For those reasons, his friends like to call him the "Sci-Fi Shakespeare Guy."

Susan Eager

Susan is little more than a figment of your imagination. You
didn't know you were so mixed up inside, did you? Susan
suggests that you seek help for your hallucinations, or at the
very least, consult with your therapist about why you would
create an attractive and intelligent, but nonetheless fictional,
skilled author. There is nothing more important than your
mental health and stability.

Carolee Eubanks

Carolee Eubanks is an enigma, managing to be both horribly over-scheduled and horribly under-employed at the same time. She holds an MBA and years of defense contracting expertise that she is currently not utilizing in the least, but she has been a successful independent consultant for the last eight years. Recently, she has spent a lot of time responding to contest challenges on a Web site called Take180.com, where she is willing to make a complete fool of herself for cash and prizes. Her husband, two small children, and cat are not only supportive of this venture, they actually participate in her shenanigans. She considers herself very fortunate.

Sally Jean Genter

Sally Jean Genter, known as dr.jean and JeanTre16 within certain online writing communities, resides in beautiful North Carolina and holds a B.A. from the University of Hawaii. She works in the field of education and has written numerous stories, poems, and screenplays. In addition to placing finalist in the 2007 Kirk versus Picard screenwriters' contest, her short fictional piece, *Dream Cycles*, won the 2008 Wake: Dream Writers contest, sponsored by Simon & Schuster and FanLib.com. Outside of working and writing, she devotes time to her family, church, and cat, not necessarily in that order.

⚷

Leila McNamara

Leila McNamara is a college student who has been writing passionately (some might say obsessively) for the last decade. She currently lives in Virginia, but was born on the West Coast and raised mainly in the Midwest. Encouraged by her visits to Disneyland as a child, Leila's imagination is working constantly. As a loyal Star Trek fan, Leila found herself on the fandom Web site FanLib.com as Leila_Data, where she discovered others who shared her passion and talent for writing. Leila's free time (when not used for writing) is spent drawing, reading, and hanging out with friends.

D.G. McMurry Jr.

D.G. McMurry Jr. (aka dgtrekker) has spent most of his life wandering the Arizona desert. He has been creating since an early age. He has won various awards and accolades for his works. D.G. has had both his art and writing published in newspapers, trade publications, and magazines. His love of *Star Trek* drew him to join a close gathering of friends that would eventually become the G10 Group, and the same love of *Trek* has also made him a Greater Deity (so far) in *Star Trek* trivia. He can frequently be found hiding around the 'net and is usually at his blog: http://www.webjam.com/dgtrekkers_hangout/.

Steve Boudreault

Steve (aka Tribblemaker) is a copyeditor, writer, and all-around word nerd. He lives in Danvers, Massachusetts, on the grounds of what was once the Danvers State Insane Asylum. He's not yet possessed, but hopes to be soon. Steve has been writing short stories for as long as he can remember, and some of them were actually not horrible. *Keys* is Steve's second collaboration with G10, but by no means his last. There are four lights.

8—⊤

194

Chris Whigham

Chris Whigham resides in the Commonwealth of Kentucky, and often draws upon his Midwest upbringing for inspiration. His stories are usually full of real characters with relevant issues, and almost always a touch of humor. His motto? "If it's too serious to laugh at, then you really have a problem!" After publishing *The Artifact: An Anthology* with his fellow G10 members, writing has become a passion for Chris rather than a mere hobby, and he looks forward to many more book projects. Chris lives with his wife, Shannon, and his dog, Ben, and is active at LifePointe Church in Louisville.

⌐⌐

Sheri McMurray

Sheri McMurray is thankful for her family, first for being patient when she was deeply absorbed in her selfish craft of writing, and second for always being there to read, review, and encourage. Thirdly, there seems always to be unsung influences in the life of anyone who creates. People who inadvertently inspire or encourage the person creating to go that extra mile. It is the inspiration of lifelong friend Cathy Shelton, as well as the tutelage of gifted artist John Richter, that Sheri owes a heartfelt debt of gratitude. Without Cathy's devotion, chapter three of *The Artifact: An Anthology* would never have been penned. Without John's guidance, the artwork that graces that work as well as this book you now hold, *Keys ... Unlocking the Universe*, would have remained a dream never crafted, a door never unlocked. Ultimately life's hallways are constantly branching in many directions. There have been doors opened, rooms explored, and many doors yet to open. Sheri has in her life the master keys to open untold doors. Those keys are the love of her husband, Richard, and her steadfast faith. Here we are at the close of 2008. As the holidays become ever near, Sheri and the nine authors she has grown to love as family prepare to put this, their second effort, to press. There is no doubt the keys have been turned, the doors have been opened to ever new possibilities, and that this is the time to be truly thankful.

⌐━⌐